AUTUMN CRUSH

A ROSEDALE NOVEL

ELLE WATERS

For my Grandma Lynn

ONE
DREW

I'M LATE.

Alyson's going to kill me. She's not only the best assistant editor I've ever worked with, she's the most punctual person I've ever met. But I just couldn't make the morning happen.

Ironically enough, I woke up before my alarm, with Cinnamon, the marmalade cat I inherited from my dad along with this rambling farmhouse, kneading his paws on my chest until I opened my eyes. But once I shuffled out of bed, a truly catastrophic number of unfortunate events conspired against me. The shower ran cold—again—so I had to call the plumber, and then somehow my oatmeal managed to burn, overflow the pot, and gum up the stove all at once. Then I couldn't find my slippers—it turned out Cinnamon was using them for a cat bed.

Alyson's on California time, but she's still in our video chat before I sit down at my desk, finishing what little oatmeal I could salvage, feeling like the kid from that children's book about the no-good, very bad day.

"I'm late. I know I'm late," I say before she can berate me.

"Hey, you're the one who'll look bad if we don't finish the rough cut." Her short brown fringe of hair has new pink highlights, and she's wearing different hexagonal glasses over her brown eyes.

"I'm the editor. I'll just blame it on my assistant. Nice hair, by the way," I slip in. "New glasses?"

"Ha ha. Yeah. I decided to change it up."

"You having a date later doesn't have anything to do with it?"

"Ugh. I never should have told you about that." She groans and covers her face with her hands.

"What? I'm just happy for you. You've been working too much lately. You're too young to turn into a workaholic."

"Like you, you mean?"

I find a spot for my empty oatmeal bowl on the cluttered desktop. "I'm not a workaholic, I'm just bad at time management. It's not the same thing." And it makes me sound marginally less pathetic.

"That's what you have me for. You make the genius editing decisions, and I make sure we deliver the cuts on time."

I grin at her through the magic of computers. "What would I do without you?"

"Let's not find out," she says, winking at me. We spend the next hour getting organized to tackle act three of this project. It's a feature, a queer indie horror film with festival aspirations. The script is better than average. I've worked with the producer before, but never this director. Phoebe doesn't always understand that I can't put in shots she didn't actually film, but we're only a few weeks out from delivering a rough cut, and I can feel it coming together. It's exciting.

Alyson organizes the footage, syncs the audio and video, prepares the projects for me to work on, and exports screeners of our cuts while I do the creative editing in the edit bay I set up on the first floor of the farmhouse. My dad had used the small windowless room for an office. Once I realized the task of sorting through my father's stuff and getting the farmhouse ready for sale wasn't exactly a one-weekend project, I replaced his old wobbly wooden desk with a sturdy metal one, and brought my gear, computer, and monitors from L.A.

In fact, I've been here for close to six months, and the real estate agent's card my dad's lawyer handed me has been buried under so much paperwork that at this point I'm not sure I could even find it again. Those months have been filled with maintenance since something always seems to be breaking in this old place. I bought a new fridge when the old one crapped out over the Fourth of July. The plumber's been here what seems like every month for various leaks and to fix the outdated water heater.

This whole place used to be part of a working farm, but all that's left is a falling down barn in an overgrown meadow and picturesque stone walls marking where fields used to be. The woods have been encroaching for years, and I kind of like it this way—the land returning to a natural state, protecting me from my neighbors, but not from the wildlife that makes its home here.

I think I see why my dad liked it here. After two decades of constantly moving, once, twice, sometimes three times a year, he finally found a place to settle down. I just wish I knew why he couldn't stay put before I left for college. Why couldn't he grow roots when I needed him to, instead of dragging me around the country with him?

Just the sight of a big cardboard box would set my heart racing. Moving was a way of life for me as a child, but I hated everything about it. The inevitable lost box with my favorite toys or books, getting used to the new smells and quirks of yet another apartment or duplex, always being the new kid in school. I was never the kind of new kid who parlayed my mysteriousness into popularity. I was always the dorky, quiet one who nobody wanted to sit with at lunch. I told myself I didn't care because I'd rather read a book or draw, anyway. And if I did actually succeed at finding a friend group, like fall of my senior year in high school, it didn't matter. He packed us up so fast I didn't even have time to say goodbye.

After college in Los Angeles, I found an apartment I liked and stayed put—until I got the out-of-the-blue call that Dad had passed from a heart attack. In a daze, I organized a surprisingly well-attended funeral—it seemed my loner father was able to make friends once he settled down. I also had to make some decisions about the estate. It was depressingly easy to pick up stakes in a city I'd lived in for over a decade. I still have the lease on my apartment, but there's a letter somewhere in the growing pile on the desk asking if I'm going to give it up once and for all.

Another question I wish I knew the answer to.

"So you ready for Charles later?" Alyson asks as we end our meeting.

"Yep—clean sheets on the bed and everything."

"Thanks for doing this."

"Sure," I say with more casualness than I feel. When Alyson asked me if her brother could basically move into my guest house for a few weeks, I was too surprised to come up with a convincing reason to say no. My dad had listed the guest house on those temporary vacation rental sites. The income had helped supplement his retirement funds. After he died, I canceled the handful of remaining bookings and added that rental to the list of things I'd think about later. But it's a nice little place—a single bedroom, a small but functional kitchen combined with a multipurpose room. It only needed to be aired out after a hot, humid summer. I had it cleaned and stocked with a few essentials for Charles, Alyson's brother. She told me he lives in the city, and he needs a place to stay while he organizes a charity bike race that's going to be held in Rosedale later this fall, but that's the extent of it.

I've gotten too used to my own company. It'll probably be good for me to have another human being in my orbit—one I don't see on a computer screen.

"Then I'll see you tomorrow," Alyson says. "Unless something comes up."

"Enjoy your date." She's got her to-do list, and I've got mine. We usually only meet in the morning, then spend the day getting our work done.

She scrunches up her face as if disgusted I even brought it up, then smiles, says "Thanks," and logs off.

I usually enjoy working independently and have no trouble sinking into the intense focus editing requires, but today I'm distractible. Every thirty minutes I pull off my headphones, wondering if I've heard the door.

I have Charles's phone number, but all the arrangements have been made through Alyson. All I know is he's arriving by train in the early afternoon. I experience a moment of panic. I should have asked more questions. What if he's annoying or weird or homophobic?

The shrill ring of the old-fashioned doorbell gets my blood pumping, and I leap from my desk. Finally, I'll get to meet the mysterious Charles. But standing on my front step is just the plumber, a young guy who probably makes more in a month than I do in a year. His van is parked in the wide area off to the side of the house next to my hybrid sedan, which I drove here from Los Angeles with my editing equipment. It still has California plates.

"Hey Lucas," I say. "You remember where the boiler is?"

"Yep. Let me go check it out." He knows where the stairs to the basement are, so I let him do his thing. My concentration is shot—might as well have lunch.

I'm microwaving leftovers when Lucas bounds up the stairs, sending Cinnamon skittering. "Need a part from my van." I follow him to the door, and my eye catches something moving up the long driveway from the street. It's a man on a bicycle.

My first thought is bike messenger, but who would make deliveries on a bike in rural Connecticut? As he comes closer, I notice he's got a large backpack on, and his bike has saddlebags. I look at his face, but he's wearing a helmet and wraparound shades. I can't make out most of his features, but he has a strong, stubble-covered jaw.

When he's about twenty feet away, he seems to see me watching from the door and lifts a bike-gloved hand in greeting. I wave back, a prickle of awareness at the back of my brain. I don't know him, this guy wearing tight-fitting nylon shorts and a blue T-shirt that clings to his chest and arms. But there's something familiar about him.

"Charles?" I ask when he's close enough to the house to unclip his bike shoes from the pedals and swing himself over the seat, walking his bike the last few feet to the stone slab front steps.

"Yeah. Well, Charlie. Allie's the only one who calls me Charles."

It's the voice that does it. I know that voice—a clear and friendly tenor. And the name. I didn't know Charles, but I know—or rather knew—Charlie. Charlie Linden, not Cross, which is Alyson's last name. Could Charles Cross, the man I was expecting, actually be Charlie Linden, my friend for about three months during my senior year of high school? I rack my brain, but I'm almost completely certain Charlie had been an only child, like me. It was one of the reasons we became friends, both latchkey kids with single parents who worked late, leaving us plenty of time for hanging out and watching movies after school.

I haven't seen him in fifteen years. It's probably not the same guy.

It couldn't be.

But then he sets his bike against the big rhododendron to the left of the front steps, unsnaps his helmet, whips off his sporty sunglasses, and I know. It's him.

"Drew, right?" He smiles at me, revealing the crooked bottom tooth I knew would be there, and it's as if not a day has passed since I last saw him.

"That's me." I search for a smile, but the one that lands on my face feels foreign and ill-fitting.

We shake hands when he scales the steps and offers me his. The touch lasts for two seconds; forgettable, but I could never forget the man standing in front of me. He has the same warm brown eyes and the same cheerful smile of seventeen-year-old Charlie. He looks older, of course, way more solid under his skintight biking clothes, stubble instead of peach fuzz lining his square jaw. The last time I saw him was fifteen years ago. I was always angry about something back then, but never with Charlie, who was a beacon of light—the reason to get up in the morning and trundle to school, the reason to go to our mutual friend Paloma's house to watch cult movies in her basement, the reason I was absolutely 100 percent sure I was gay, because back then I wanted to kiss Charlie Linden more than anything in the world.

He was my first crush.

My first heartache.

He looks at me and I wait for him to say something like, "Oh my gosh—aren't you Andy, the kid I hung out with for a few months before you just disappeared over winter break? I heard you moved to Indiana or something."

And I'd say, "Illinois," and explain how my dad moved us around so much that sometimes I didn't have a chance to say goodbye to whatever friends I might have made. That when I went to college I left the name Andy behind and started calling myself Drew. That I grew three inches in six months, didn't stop growing until I hit six feet, and never quite lost the awkwardness of being suddenly tall and gangly after a lifetime of being short and chubby.

In my dream movie version of this unlikely scenario, he'd tell me he's been searching for me all these years and now that he's finally found me, he's never letting me go.

But life, as I discover over and over again, is not a movie.

All he says is, "This is a beautiful spot. Thanks for having me. I know Allie kind of twisted your arm." There's no recognition in his eyes. No spark of awareness. Just bland politeness and perhaps some unease at my apparent inability to communicate.

I clear my throat. Now would be the time, wouldn't it? To mention that we already know each other. But that would open up a vein to my—our—past. Who wants to talk about the bad old days of high school? I purposefully changed the minute I got my diploma, reinventing myself the way I never was able to when moving to a new town. I didn't look back. I don't really want to now.

Besides, what if he doesn't remember me because I'm just not that memorable? Those three months have always existed in my mind as an unusually happy, if long-ing-filled, time. Better to keep all that in the past.

Then again, it would be weird not to say something, even if it might make things awkward. I open my mouth, only for Lucas to trudge up from his truck carrying a wrench and a clear plastic bag with some kind of white elbow joint in it.

"You find what you need?" I ask Lucas, cowardly latching onto the interruption.

"Think so. Give me a little longer," Lucas says. He nods to Charlie, who nods back, then moves past me into the house.

There's a tense pause I don't fill with revelations. "Well," I say, "let me show you the guest house."

If Charlie Linden doesn't remember me, I guess we're starting over.

TWO
CHARLIE

I PICK up my bike and follow my host from the front of his charming dark gray house with its red door and white trim to a brown wooden structure that's to the left and a little bit behind the main house.

"It was a milking shed about a hundred years ago," Drew says as we approach the building. "Over time, it was converted to a woodshed, then a guest house. If you're missing anything you need, just let me know."

He uses a key from his keyring to open the door. "Damn, I forgot your set in the house." He gives me a vaguely apologetic smile. He's got a nice face—a strong, slightly wide nose, clear gray eyes, thick dark eyebrows, and curly, or maybe just messy, almost-black hair. He looks pale, though, like he hasn't seen the sun in weeks. He's at least as tall as my six feet, but the arms coming out of his polo shirt are thin, matching his overall lanky build. I'm usually more attracted to guys who are athletic, like me, but there's something about him that makes me look twice.

My sister didn't mention that her boss was quietly attractive. She also didn't tell me if he was into men, but I do remember her saying he's not in a relationship. Her exact words were, "human interaction will be good for him." I'd been too busy in the run-up to boarding the train for Rosedale to think much about the man I'm renting a guest house from for a month, but if I had I wouldn't have pictured someone so young. He can't be older than his early thirties, like me.

We walk through the main room, which has a tiny couch, a coffee table, and a small TV on a stand, and leads into an open kitchen.

"There's basic cookware, but no dishwasher, I'm afraid," Drew says.

"No worries. I don't mind getting my hands dirty." I hold them up, realize I'm still wearing my bike gloves, and take them off.

He smiles, making his face crease. He's even cuter when he smiles. "I didn't expect you to show up on a bike. I had the impression you were taking a train."

"I did take the train." I stuff the gloves in an outer pocket of my backpack and then set the pack on the ground out of the way. "I brought my bike on board, then biked from the station."

"What's that—five miles?"

"Six. A nice little warm-up." It felt amazing, despite the unseasonal heat of the late September day, to be biking somewhere where there were more trees than people. I vow to take advantage of the quiet country roads to bike as much as I can while I'm in Rosedale. I wonder idly if Drew rides.

"Here's the bedroom," he says, opening one of the interior doors.

Right, I should be paying attention to my new home for the next month. I peek around him and see a simple but clean room with a queen-size bed done up in white linens.

"This is great. Really nice. Allie says you haven't lived here very long."

Drew leaves the bedroom door open and walks back to the main room. I follow. The guest house isn't huge, but it feels airy with its high ceilings and white painted walls. It's certainly more spacious than my six-hundred-foot studio apartment in the city. I pay for the location, which is steps from the Hudson River Greenway, where I can easily ride the length of Manhattan.

When Brock was alive, we'd talked about moving in together, pooling our resources and getting something bigger. That was one of many dreams that died along with him.

"I'm sorry—I can't get over you calling her Allie. I'm pretty sure if I tried to call her that she'd quit."

I laugh. That sounds like Allie. "She is very particular. But I have big brother privileges."

A confused look crosses his face, but he simply says, "Well, I'm sure you know it's best to keep on her good side."

"Oh, that I do, intimately."

"And she's brilliant. Easily the best assistant editor I've ever worked with. She'll be running her own editing house before long."

"That sounds right." I'm glad Drew recognizes how

awesome my little sister is. "Is it difficult with her being on the West Coast?"

"It took some adjusting. But fortunately, she's an early bird and I'm a...mid-morning bird. Our schedules actually work out better now than they did when I was in L.A."

"That's lucky." I don't really understand what it is that Allie and Drew do, but I know it's creative and cool and they're good at it. Allie was a film major, then worked for another editor—who turned out to be a jerk—before she found Drew. They worked on a commercial together, and now I'm pretty sure Allie said they're editing a movie.

I look at Drew again. There's something kind of familiar about him. But maybe it's just that I'm remembering what Allie told me about their current project—that the filmmakers had tried to hire as many queer people as they could both behind and in front of the camera since it was some kind of gay slasher film. Maybe Drew *is* into guys.

Not that I'm looking.

Or maybe I am.

I don't know. It's been almost four years since Brock, and I really didn't expect it to take this long to get back into the dating scene. I've casually hooked up with a few guys since he died, but those were more flings of convenience than attempts to find a real relationship. That side of my life just hasn't been a priority. But since my last birthday, when I realized I was actually thirty-two even though I barely remember turning thirty, I've been thinking it's time to...try again? Ugh, the logistics of dating seem overwhelming, especially when I've got the logistics of a bike race to plan out. Easier to put off thinking about my personal life until after the event.

"Anyway, I'm always at home if you need anything."

"Thanks, Drew. Is it okay if I bring my bike inside?" There's a perfect spot by the front door, and the polished dark wood floors look like they can stand up to a little dirt and grease.

"Sure. Well. Have a good stay, Charlie," he says, a little stiffly.

"Thanks." I smile at him, then remember. "Oh, there is something I need from you."

He stares at me, and I swear there's a flicker of...*something* behind his pretty gray eyes. "What's that?"

"The key."

"Oh, right." He smiles a bit bashfully. "Come on over, before I forget."

I follow him back to the house. "How old is this place?"

"The farmhouse dates back to 1889. It's been added onto, and renovated a couple of times, but overall it's as creaky and drafty as it was back then, I assume. It has a lot of character."

The stone slab front steps feel solid under my feet. "I like a place that's seen it all. Makes you feel pretty safe inside."

He glances sidelong at me. "Yeah. I feel that way, too."

Drew does seem kind of rusty at the whole talking-to-people thing, but he's not a hopeless case. I know we just met, but I like him.

And I wonder exactly why Allie thought this would be the best place for me to spend my month in Rosedale.

"The keys are in here." I follow him to the kitchen, which is a mix of old scrubbed-wood countertops and newer stainless steel appliances. "Have you had lunch?"

"I had some trail mix on the train." I was too excited to see my new temporary home to stop for provisions.

"I'm going to put in a grocery order later. Feel free to add anything to the list."

"You get your groceries delivered?" I know it's pretty common, and sometimes I need to do it in the city if I'm getting too much to carry or take on my bike, but I figured out here people just fill up their cars with stuff.

He shrugs. "I get everything delivered."

"Okay, that would be great. I'm all about using my bike for transportation, but sometimes grocery shopping is a pain."

"I bet. I can offer you some leftovers." He looks at the fridge doubtfully.

"Don't worry about it. I'll get settled and then ride into town." I mapped out the route beforehand. It's about three miles from Drew's place to the nearest grocery store, but less than two to Rosedale's downtown. I've been to the town twice before, once for my friend Jack Avery's housewarming party and once for his wedding to Pete Blekitny, and I remember the downtown stretch being bike-friendly and having plenty of places for a hungry bachelor to eat.

"Wow, so you're really into biking," Drew says.

I have to laugh at the understatement. "Yeah, I really am," I say. "It's a big part of who I am. Do you ride?"

He shakes his head quickly, then says, "Well, I know *how* to ride a bicycle. I just don't do it very often. Like... ever. I think there's an old bike in the barn. My dad left a lot of stuff behind that I haven't had a chance to go through yet."

"An old bike?" I've been getting interested in vintage bikes lately. I don't have room for a collection in my place in the city, but I love the way a well-built bike will last forever if you keep taking care of it. "What kind?"

He laughs. "I have no idea. You're welcome to take a look. Maybe you could tell me if it's worth keeping or not."

"I'll do that." I catch his gaze, but he immediately looks away. There's something about him I can't put my finger on. We just met, but it's like he reminds me of someone I know, only I can't make the connection. A handsome orange cat strolls into the room. "Who's this?"

"This is Cinnamon. I didn't name him. He's another thing my dad left behind. One of the best things, actually. Hope you're not allergic."

"I love cats," I say, dropping to my knees and holding out my hand. Cinnamon sniffs the air around me, blinks, then, to my utter delight, comes close enough for me to rub his back. "I had a cat growing up." Brock was allergic, so there was a time I thought my cat-owning days were behind me.

"He's a good one," Drew says, smiling down at us. "He likes you."

I continue to stroke Cinnamon for another twenty seconds, then he jumps onto the island and begins cleaning his paws.

Drew drags a shallow bowl filled with different sets of keys across the counter toward him. "Alyson says you're planning some kind of a bike event?" He comes up with a single key that's attached to a bottle opener doubling as a key chain and hands it to me.

"Yep, it's a fundraiser and a memorial ride. My boyfriend, who was an avid cyclist, died from a rare complication of Lyme disease, so I'm raising money for Lyme disease awareness and prevention. It's a ten-mile group ride, then we'll have a series of amateur races for different age groups downtown." I know the spiel by heart, since I've used it so often in my cold calls to companies asking for donations and support. I do marketing as my job, so the elevator pitch comes fairly easily to me. But Drew's face changes as I talk—maybe he's put off by my casually mentioning Brock and his death. It's been nearly four years, but I still have to paper over how much it still hurts, or I'd never get through the first sentence of my little speech.

He looks like he's trying to decide what to say, and for a second I'm afraid he's going to be an asshole about the boyfriend thing and disappoint me. But he only says, "I'm sorry for your loss," his voice respectfully low.

My chest aches. Not with disappointment, no—Drew passed that test—but with sorrow that never completely goes away, and gratefulness for the small human comfort in his words.

"Thanks." We make eye contact for a brief moment before he looks away. I turn the key in my hands, then remember that I'm paying him for a place to live, not to be my friend. "Anyway, I should probably get going. I'm interrupting your work, and I want to get settled in."

"Right. Of course. You'll want to unpack," Drew says, as if he's been far away and my words remind him to come back to earth.

He walks me to the door, and I try to read the shift in his mood. "See you around, Drew."

"Okay."

I'm down the front steps and a dozen feet toward the guest house when he calls out to me. "Charlie?"

I turn, and he's leaning against the doorjamb. The afternoon sun is beginning to throw shadows, but I can still make out his appealing face. "Yeah?"

There's a pause, and then he says, "Text me your grocery order and I'll put it in tonight."

I nod and turn my back on my curious landlord, the niggling feeling of missing something following me all the way home.

THREE
DREW

LUCAS RETURNS FROM THE BASEMENT, declares victory against the old pipes and the ancient water heater, and tells me that next time he might have to replace the whole thing.

"You should really consider getting a tankless unit," he says. "Endless hot water and more energy efficient, too."

"I'll think about it." Investing in the house like that only makes sense if I'm going to stay here long term.

By the time I write Lucas a check with the chicken scratch I call handwriting and sit back down at my desk it's nearly three. I'm totally behind on today's schedule, which is not atypical. I'll make it up by working through dinner, which is what I usually end up doing.

But my concentration never recovers after the twin—triplet?—revelations that the occupant of the guest house is Charlie Linden, and that he had a boyfriend. Who died.

God, I don't know how long it's been, but the grief still residing in his warm brown eyes was unmistakable. From the little he told me, it sounds like the death was unexpected, and maybe preventable, and while it's not the same, it reminds me how sudden my dad's passing was. Some days I still forget he's gone, that I'm not just visiting him in this place that he loved so much. Some days the grief makes me wish I'd never decided to come here, with all the reminders of him.

So Charlie lost someone, and it's clearly still fresh.

But the fact that his someone was a guy—holy shit.

All I can think is that Paloma was right.

She's the only one I told I had a crush on Charlie back in the day. And she's the one who insisted I should say something to him. I thought she was delusional.

If I was editing a movie about my life, the year I was seventeen would be a montage showing a dorky film nerd finding his footing at yet another new school. Dad moved us to West Hartford. Hall High School wasn't so bad. And I had first period with a kid named Charlie Linden.

He was the first real boy I ever had a crush on. Zac Efron doesn't count. I'd look forward to going to school just so I could spend economics class staring at the back of his head from two rows of desks away.

I was content to live in peace with my little unrequited crush. But then something happened.

We became friends.

Technically, I became friends with Paloma first, because we were both into *Mystery Science Theater* 3000 and Adult Swim, and she was already friends with Charlie. The third member of their little group was Seb, who had a thing for Paloma, but was clearly never going to do anything about it. That year, somehow, I became the fourth member of their crew, for once in my life having people to eat lunch with and invite over to watch late night television in the living room of the furnished apartment Dad rented in town.

Charlie was, in a boring but accurate word, nice. He never seemed awkward the way I constantly was. He'd sit next to me on the couch, throw his arm around my shoulders, turn to me with a smile that showed off his crooked bottom tooth. He didn't mean anything by it, obviously.

But then Paloma ruined it by telling me I should say something to him.

"What do you mean?" I hedged.

"You like him, right?" She was a skinny girl with long arms and legs, and black hair that hung to her waist.

"Don't be ridiculous," I'd scoffed unconvincingly.

"You should ask him on a date."

"But we're friends."

"And you could be making out," she'd said.

I couldn't form a sentence that would convey how incredibly far out of the realm of possibility that was. I hated her a little for planting the idea in my head that something so farfetched could ever happen, and I resented her for shoving my private fantasy crush on Charlie into the messy, dangerous real world.

A crush on Zac Efron was safely theoretical. I'd never have the opportunity to meet the *High School Musical* star, so who cared if anyone knew I thought he was dreamy? Charlie was different. Even though I had zero chance of being with him, just like Zac, our friends knowing I liked him suddenly seemed a liability I couldn't afford. What if Charlie found out? Would our friendship be over?

In the end, it didn't matter, because I never had to risk ruining everything by telling him about my crush. Over Christmas break, Dad got a job in Chicago, and we were gone by New Year's. Charlie was in Vermont, skiing with his mom, and I never got to say goodbye. I never saw him again.

Until he rode a bicycle up my driveway and back into my life earlier today.

And I punked out yet again by not even telling him who I am—or rather, who I was.

Truth is stranger than fiction, yes, and in someone's unsold screenplay there might be a meet-cute like this, but it doesn't matter—even if I'm the right gender for him to possibly be attracted to, life isn't a movie, and someone like Charlie Linden would never be interested in someone like me.

With difficulty, I settle my headphones over my ears and get back to work.

I'VE CUT TOGETHER the next minute of film when my phone buzzes on my desk, startling me out of the deep focus I enter when editing takes over my brain.

It's a text. From Charlie. Well, in my phone he's still Charles, the way Alyson shared his contact information, so I change his listing to Charlie. Charles sounds like a stuffy stockbroker, and Charlie Linden, with his crooked bottom tooth and penchant for bike riding, is the opposite of stuffy.

> If you haven't ordered the groceries yet, here are a few things I could use.

He follows with a short list of staples, but one item on the list catches my eye and makes me laugh. One thing I remember teenage Charlie always having in his backpack was a bag of gummy bears. Apparently, he hasn't outgrown the habit. I can't resist calling him out.

> Gummy bears?

A minute later, he replies.

> They're my one vice.

> Maybe you should get two bags.

I chuckle to myself, save my project, and put in the grocery order, including two bags of gummy bears. At the last minute, I up the order to three bags—including one for me. I choose the earliest delivery window I can.

> Groceries will be here tomorrow afternoon.

> Thanks. Let me know what I owe you.

> I'll just add it to your rent.

> Sounds good.

I stare at the phone for a minute, wondering what I could possibly say to prolong this scintillating text exchange, when I remember I shouldn't want to prolong it. Charlie's just a tenant, not a friend.

But as I try to get back into the edit, I wonder if maybe he could be. Again.

FOUR
DREW

I'M ACTUALLY on time for my morning meeting with Alyson, logging on five whole seconds before she does. Last night I worked until after nine, then had trouble falling asleep, wondering how Charlie was doing in the guest house. He'd texted me one more time last night to say he'd ordered "too much takeout" so not to worry when the delivery guy came. I'd written back that he was free to have visitors or deliveries or whatever. It didn't occur to me until much later that maybe he was hinting at wanting company for dinner.

Oh well, being socially hopeless is the reason I'm in this stupid situation in the first place. I can't tell Alyson I already know her brother, because then she'll tell him and it'll be a thing.

"Morning, Drew." Alyson sounds even more chipper than usual, and I remember she had her date last night.

"Date went well, I take it?" I sip my coffee and wait for the download.

"Date went very well, but I don't want to jinx it," she says.

"That's all I'm going to get? You've been talking about this guy for a month."

"That was when he was just my barista crush. Now he's Finn and we're maybe going out again this weekend. How'd it go with my brother?"

If she's got her mind set on something, nothing I can say will change it, so I don't bother, and I take the shift in topic in stride.

"He's all settled in, I think." I can't tell her about the weird coincidence of me already knowing him, but maybe she can shed some light on a few things. "He told me about his boyfriend who died. How horrible."

"He told you about Brock?"

"He mentioned it when he was explaining about the bike event. It's a fundraiser?"

"Yeah. He died about four years ago. Brock was this healthy, active guy. He'd been on a hiking trip on the Appalachian Trail a few months earlier, and then one day he just dropped dead. The doctors said it was a rare heart condition caused by Lyme disease—at least that's what they think it was. It's all a little fuzzy. But it really wrecked Charles. They were together for a few years. He's been putting this event together for a long time, and then finally decided to do it in Rosedale because his friend Jack lives there and he's one of the big sponsors."

"So he's gay?"

"Charles? Yeah, like super gay. Didn't I mention that?" She looks at me through the screen, and I can't tell if she's faking surprise or not.

"You didn't. Not that it matters." It doesn't. It only means that everything I told myself when I was seventeen and crushing on my straight friend turned out not to be true.

"He's gay and single. Just like you," she says casually. Too casually.

"Alyson."

"Yes?"

"Please tell me you aren't trying to matchmake us."

"I'm not trying to matchmake you," she says solemnly. Then she bursts out giggling.

"Oh my god, you *are* trying to set us up." Now I get it —the insistence that I reopen the guest house for this special occasion, her checking and double-checking that I'd be there to greet him. "You little minx."

"Honestly, he needed a place to stay, and he didn't want to impose on his friend Jack for a whole month or stay in a hotel all that time. I just thought you two might get along."

"In what reality would Charlie and I be a good fit? I'm a film nerd with a Vitamin D deficiency and he's a—"

"A what?"

I choose my words carefully. "A guy who brings a bicycle on a train and has a gummy bear addiction."

Her eyebrows rise comically high. "Seems like you're already getting to know *Charlie* pretty well."

"That's not the point."

"What is the point, Drew? Besides, you're selling yourself completely short. You're smart, successful, interesting, and attractive if you like soulful eyes and messy hair. Which Charles does, I promise."

I think this is her version of a compliment. There's no way Charlie thinks I'm attractive. "Look, I appreciate that you care about me, but relationships don't just happen because two people who have the right combination of body parts meet each other."

"Not true. Do you know the statistics of married couples who were introduced by mutual friends? It's high, Drew. It's high."

I sigh, worn down by her twenty-three-year-old's optimism. "I'm not going to win this argument with you, but—"

"See? I told you, you're smart!" She interrupts me, triumphant. "Charles would be lucky to land a guy like you."

"Can we just stop talking about this?" I plead. "We do have actual work to get done."

"Oh, right, boss. Of course, boss," she says sassily. "Did you see Phoebe's notes on the hot tub scene?"

"Not yet. So you can prep the park scene, and I'll sift through Phoebe's notes." We talk shop for another minute, then something horrifying occurs to me. "Oh god —you didn't tell Charlie about the matchmaking thing, did you?"

What if the entire time we were interacting yesterday he knew his sister was trying to get us together? How mortifying.

"No, of course not," Alyson says quickly. "I just thought if I got you two in the same place, maybe something would happen, you know, organically."

I groan. "Okay, I'm going to forget we had this conversation. I will treat Charlie exactly like I have been

—as the renter of my guest house. And you aren't going to tell him we talked about this, either. Are you?"

She squints at me. "I don't want to make a promise I can't keep."

"Alyson!" I wail. "Seriously. If this comes up, you have to make it completely clear that it was all your idea, and I had nothing to do with it."

"Dude, chill," she says with heat. "I'm not going to give you credit for my idea. Besides, Charles won't say anything about it to me. He's kind of private about his dating life. I don't even know if he's seen anyone since Brock died. It's sad, actually. He's got so much love to give and nowhere to put it."

I'm almost taken in by her monologue. "Okay, that's enough of the sob story."

The faux tragic edge disappears from her voice. "No, really. He's lonely. I thought maybe you could be friends, if nothing else."

I take my glasses off and rub my eyes. This conversation has taken a year off my life. "Fine. Great. Let's stop talking about it."

"Fine. Great."

"Now let's get back to work."

"Already working."

THE DOORBELL RING startles me a few hours later. I look up, astonished to find I've worked straight through lunch. But I got a tricky editing sequence done, and I'm liking the way this scene is shaping up.

I go to the door, cracking my back on the way, and find the grocery delivery guy on the other side. In five minutes, the food's inside and the truck is trundling back down the long driveway.

I stick a frozen pasta dish in the microwave for my belated meal. While it heats, I put away the groceries, setting aside Charlie's order. The sight of gummy bears makes me smile. I stick one bag in my snack cupboard and place the other two in a paper bag alongside Charlie's eggs, butter, deli meat, and bread.

I debate texting to have him come pick up his stuff, but in the end, I decide to simply walk it over. I scarf down my subpar Chicken Alfredo, glance at myself in the spotted mirror in the hallway on my way out the door. I set the grocery bag down on the floor so I can run my fingers through my tangle of hair, trying to find something desirable in the face that stares back at me.

I don't spend a lot of time looking in the mirror. I hated my adolescent self, round face, pimples, too big nose. Just when I'd finally given up on matching my six-foot-tall father, I shot up, but never managed to put any more weight on my new, stretched-out frame. My face got more angular; my pimples cleared up. But I still look at myself and see a painfully gawky kid, who's better off sequestered inside, working alone.

Over the years it's gotten easier and easier to keep myself apart from the world, only texting with friends, having work meetings online, getting all my basic needs delivered right to my apartment, and now this house. Staying in my comfort zone is so much easier than the messiness of life.

It's not like I've never had a relationship. In L.A., I mostly dated other below the line guys—a composer, a set decorator, an animator. I stayed in my lane—creative guys with a thread of insecurity making them willing to date someone like me. I didn't fall madly in love with any of them, but we had some nice times. I was raised by movies, where love is usually portrayed as shockingly toxic or unrealistically passionate. I know the truth probably lies somewhere in the middle, but I might still be holding out for the kind of cinematic romance that doesn't truly exist.

Maybe by holding out for it, I don't have to try to make a real relationship work.

I stick my tongue out at my reflection. Who cares what I look like? Alyson might think all it takes two gay guys is to get within sniffing distance of each other, but that's not reality. Besides, Charlie is too much like the hot, muscular, fake-tan, teeth-whitened wannabe actors who would never give me the time of day back in L.A. He's in an entirely different bracket.

But he's lonely, Alyson's voice whispers in the back of my head as I make the short walk to the guest house, groceries in hand, a bit surprised at how dark the clouds have gotten since this morning dawned partly sunny and cool. I should be friendly to him, at least.

My resolve to offer friendship to Charlie lasts right up until he opens the door to my knock.

Shirtless.

FIVE

DREW

MY MOUTH GOES dry as I take in the expanse of firm pecs, small dark pink nipples, barely-there blond chest hair leading down to flat abs, the hair growing denser where it disappears into the waistband of his nylon athletic shorts.

I blink and return my gaze to his face, where he's smiling at me with that familiar golden retriever energy. I will my mouth to form words besides *Charlie. Hot. Want.*

"Hey, grocery delivery," I say finally.

"Thanks. I could have come over." He takes the bag from me and leaves the door open, which I take as an invitation to follow him inside. His bike is taking up space just inside the door, and he has a computer open on the kitchen table, but there's not much else of him in the small space. Makes sense, since there's only so much he could fit inside the saddlebags and backpack he arrived with yesterday.

"Sleep okay?" I ask, then wince. Now that I know

Alyson was trying to set us up, I'm even more self-conscious about what comes out of my mouth.

"Slept great," he says cheerfully as he takes his items out of the bag. The muscles in his back flex distractingly as he moves. "Really comfortable bed."

"That's good to know. I've never tried it." I immediately want to bash my head against the wooden table. "I mean, my dad used to have this place listed on short-term rental sites, but I haven't wanted to deal with all of that, so I don't really know. But it's good. That you slept well."

He puts a jar of peanut butter on the counter. "You mentioned your dad yesterday—this was his place?"

I take a breath. Okay. I can do this. I can have a normal conversation with a handsome, shirtless man. "Yeah. He died about eight months ago, left it to me."

"Oh, I'm sorry for your loss," Charlie says quietly, an echo of my words to him yesterday.

I acknowledge the sentiment with a nod of my head. "I thought I'd sell, but I haven't made a lot of progress going through his stuff. And I'm kind of starting to like it here."

He gestures toward the window above the kitchen sink with its view of the woods. "I can see why. It's beautiful. Private. I went on a walk this morning—you're pretty far from your neighbors."

"Parts of the farm got sold off over the years, and now this parcel is six acres, I think?"

"Nice." He sets deli meat, the loaf of bread, and mustard on the kitchen counter. "I'm going to make myself a sandwich. Want one?"

"No thanks, I just ate."

"Took a peek inside the barn. Some really cool old tools in there." He sets about making a simple sandwich while he talks.

"My dad was a bit of a yard sale addict in his later years. For a single guy with no grandchildren, he had way too much stuff. I should probably just rent a dumpster, but I feel bad not going through things first."

"Found the bike you mentioned—don't get rid of that," Charlie says, licking a glob of mustard from his thumb. I track the motion, feeling vaguely jealous of a condiment. "It needs a little TLC, but it would be a great bike for tooling around town in."

"Really? I wonder if there's a bike repair shop in Rosedale." I haven't spent all that much time exploring the town.

"Nearest one is in Midville," Charlie says. "They're one of the sponsors of the bike event. But I could probably do it for you, if you want. Spruce it up, I mean."

"Really?"

"I have some basic tools with me. Oh—and chain lube. I have some, but you'll want your own supply. I can text you a link to a brand I like."

"Chain lube?" Is he messing with me?

"Yeah, you don't want your chain to dry out. Gotta keep it lubed." He appears to be perfectly serious.

"Okay. Thanks," I manage to say.

He bites into his sandwich and says with his mouth full, "No problem. You need a helmet, too, if you want to ride."

"I'll add it to the list." I'm pretty proud of myself for keeping up my end of the conversation with a shirtless

Charlie when I realize I have no idea what to say next. A rumble of thunder gives me an opening. "We're in for some rain, I guess."

He looks out the window just as drops start to fall. He frowns. "Yeah. The downside of only having a bike for transportation."

"Were you going somewhere?"

"I need to pick up something at one of the businesses in town. But I can use a car service. Or my friend Jack said he could give me a ride if he gets some notice. He's a writer, so he's got a flexible schedule."

"What does he write?"

"He's got this book series for kids. Middle schoolers, actually. It's called Super Rupert, and his husband does the illustrations. You should check them out sometime."

So Charlie's friends with a gay couple who live in Rosedale, Alyson characterized him as "super gay," and I haven't been honest with him about who I am, or even told him that I'm gay, too, which is honestly simple politeness.

Only how to put it? *Hey, Charlie, I'm actually a kid you used to hang out with and I didn't mention it because deep down I'm still an insecure seventeen-year-old? And by the way, I'm gay, too. What a coincidence!*

Ugh. I'm an editor, not a writer. No writer would come up with a plot this stupid.

Another roll of thunder breaks my concentration, such as it is, and I blurt out the first thing I think of.

"Did you know Alyson was trying to matchmake us?"

SIX

CHARLIE

"SHE WHAT NOW?" I swallow the last of my sandwich and reach for my water bottle.

Drew's pale face tinges pink, and he shrugs faux-casually. He's a nice guy, but he doesn't always seem comfortable in his own skin.

"She told me this morning that she thought we might hit it off. Because I'm gay, too," he says. It doesn't come out as a confession, more of a slightly reluctant fact. "Just thought you should know. I told her she was being ridiculous—"

"Why would that be ridiculous?" I'm not a hundred percent surprised Drew is gay. My sense of that is right more often than not. Chalk it up to being a more-or-less straight-presenting jock. A guy doesn't have to be overt for me to pick up the vibe. And Drew's level of interest in my chest for the past ten minutes has given off a definite vibe—one I'm surprisingly not averse to. Which is why his immediate dismissal of the idea kind of stings.

"Oh, well. Because there's that cliché that all you

have to do is introduce two gay guys to each other and they'll hook up or whatever and I told her it doesn't work like that."

"I hear you." Clearly, Drew isn't into that scenario, but I'm a little surprised Alyson would try to put me in that situation. "Allie's never done that before," I say, refilling my water bottle at the tap. The rain's coming down harder now, beading up the small window over the sink. "I wonder why she'd get into our business like that."

"Yeah. I mean, she said something about thinking we'd get along," Drew mumbles.

"Well, she's not wrong there," I say encouragingly. "We get along. Right?"

"Sure," he says, almost grudgingly.

"And we're going to be seeing a bit of each other over the next month."

"Yes."

"Are you dating anyone?"

"Hah. No." His mouth twists as if the idea is comical to him.

"Neither am I. So we're two single gay men who get along. I'm not saying anything has to happen, but is it so wild to think that something *could* happen?"

"I guess not," he says, but it doesn't sound like he believes it.

"Unless you aren't attracted to me," I throw out, calling his bluff because I'd bet my modest 401(k) he wouldn't be this flustered if the idea of doing something with me didn't appeal to him at least a little.

"Charlie."

I like the way he says my name, almost like an endearment, if an exasperated one.

"Drew," I reply evenly.

A shadow crosses his face. "And that's another thing —I—"

A blinding flash of lightning, followed by an enormous, house-rattling boom of thunder, makes us both jump.

"Storm's right over us," I say, stating the obvious as colossal drops of rain hit the window, loud as hailstones. I cross the room to close the front door Drew left standing partially open. He moves away from me as I pass. Why is he so skittish?

The change in weather suddenly makes me aware of my lack of clothes. I stripped off my shirt after my morning walk to do my routine tick check, planning to take a shower I haven't gotten around to yet. "You better stay here until it passes."

He looks out the window, wrinkling his generous nose. "I really should get back to work."

"You'll get soaked if you go out now." The little house rattles again with another boom of thunder, proving my point.

He crosses his arms over his chest. "Fine."

I take him in; he looks more put-together today. He's wearing a long-sleeved ribbed shirt in a steel gray that complements his eyes and the dark tangle of his hair. He's got different jeans on today—these fit him better than yesterday's shapeless pair—and he's sporting new-looking sneakers that would definitely get ruined in the dash from my house to his in this downpour. I wonder if he dressed with more care today because of me and smile at the thought. He's cute. There's something about him that reminds me of someone I used to know, and it may not be fair to like Drew by association, but I'm doing it anyway.

"Let me grab a shirt," I say, passing him again. I don't touch him, though the space is small enough I could have. But I've said my piece and I'm not going to push for more.

In the bedroom, I grab a clean white T-shirt. The shower will just have to wait until later. I swipe on some deodorant in the meantime and flash a smile in the mirror to make sure I don't have anything in my teeth.

I left my phone on the top of the dresser and when I pick it up, I see a few missed messages. There's one from Jack, asking when we can get together, and one from Allie.

Just saying hi.

That one I reply to with a terse

I'll call you later.

She's got some explaining to do.

The last is from Beck, the owner of a cookie shop in town.

> I'll be in the shop until 4 today if you
> want to come and try your custom
> cookie options. I'm going away for a
> long weekend in New York tomorrow, so
> if it's not today, it'll have to wait until
> next Tuesday.

Damn. That was the errand I needed to get done this afternoon, and with the rain like it is, I'll definitely have to order a car to take me there. I go back to the living room just as another flash of lightning makes the air go white for a split second. Drew is looking out the window with the trace of a frown on his face.

"It's really coming down out there," he says, glancing over his shoulder at me. The way the light's coming in from the window highlights the angles of his face, and, again, I'm struck with a feeling of familiarity. My gut swoops unexpectedly. I feel almost like I did the first time I met Brock.

Brock had just moved to the city, and I was at Jack's pregaming before going clubbing for his birthday. Brock arrived with Jack's neighbor, Tom. Tom was the only person Brock knew in New York, so he'd tagged along in the hopes of maybe making some new friends.

The moment I saw him, all five-foot-six of him, tanned skin, short brown hair, full mouth, and sweet brown eyes, I had a feeling we were going to be important to each other. We went on our first date a week later, and we were practically inseparable after that. We never fully moved in together, but there was no rush. We thought we had all the time in the world.

Until we didn't.

Now I know that time isn't always on your side. And I know to trust my instincts.

The way I feel when I look at Drew makes me nervous. We might be at the beginning of something that's going to be awesome—or maybe I'm just confusing lust with destiny. It has been a while for me, after all, and the more I look at Drew, the more I like what I see.

I wasn't sure I'd ever feel a pull toward someone the way I felt it with Brock. I thought maybe he was it for me.

This feels the same, but different.

And either way, it scares me—because I know how painful it is when the sand runs out of the hourglass.

On the other hand, I'd like to think I've learned enough to try to take advantage of as much pleasure as I can while there's still time.

I walk right up to Drew, position myself between him and the window. I ignore the rain. I'd rather look into his storm-gray eyes.

"Hey, so I need to go into town now. I'm going to call a car—but I was thinking, if you were free, maybe we could have dinner tonight?"

I'm not surprised when he says, "I usually work through dinner." He seems like the kind of guy who talks himself out of personal situations.

I am surprised when he adds, "But I could drive you into town. And I suppose we could grab a drink or something after your errand. Or dinner. I guess."

"You wouldn't mind?" I had been angling for a date, not a ride.

"I—" He looks out the window, seemingly in a debate with himself over the answer. He looks back at me and says firmly, "No. I wouldn't mind at all. Where are we going?"

I grin, excited at the prospect of spending the rest of the day with him. "The cookie shop."

SEVEN

DREW

WHEN THE RAIN slows to a sprinkle, I dash back to my house, tell Cinnamon I'm going out for a while, grab my keys, wallet, and phone, and toss a quick text off to Allie, in case she's wondering where I am.

> Have to go offline for a bit. See you in the morning.

I turn on the do not disturb option on my phone. The last thing I need is Charlie's sister interrupting our ... run to the cookie shop? It's not exactly what I thought he meant by errand, but I'm game. When he asked me to dinner, I knew he didn't mean as friends. He meant as a possible date, depending on how things went.

And I wanted to say yes.

Besides, I know if I go back to work, I won't get anything done anyway, because I'll be overanalyzing our entire conversation and thinking about if he really meant it when he said there might be something between us.

But now I have a dilemma. I never expected the guy

renting my guest house to be Charlie, but he is, and it's weird that I haven't told him about our previous connection. I made it weird. I could just pretend to suddenly realize who he is, but that would be an actual lie, rather than just lying by omission, which is what I've been doing since the minute he arrived.

Honestly, how did I get myself into this soap opera of a situation?

Okay, we're spending the next few hours together. I give myself a deadline of telling him who I am before I drop him back at his house later today. There, I can be a grownup. Barely.

I get to my car and swear under my breath. It's a mess, as per usual, so I shovel a sweatshirt, books, half-empty reusable water bottles, and random trash from the front passenger seat to the back. I turn the car on and blast the air to get rid of the stale smell. When was the last time I even drove somewhere?

The passenger door opens and Charlie drops into the newly cleared out front seat just as I'm adjusting the stereo. It's on the local news station, so I hit the scan button until it lands on some alt rock, which feels safe. It's probably a lost cause to get Charlie to think I'm anywhere close to cool, but I feel like I have to make an effort.

"So, this cookie shop is on Main Street?" I ask as he buckles up and I head down my driveway.

"Yeah. It's pretty new. I think it only opened earlier this month. But the owner was really enthusiastic about the bike event, and he offered to make a special cookie for it, with all the profits from sales going to the fundraiser.

He said he'd give me a few options on flavors, so we're going to a tasting."

"What, like for wedding cakes?"

He laughs. "Yeah, I guess something like that."

"Fun." What a concept.

I know how to get downtown, and it's not long before I'm pulling into a street parking spot in front of Beck's Cookie Counter. The sign looks new, a dark blue wood shingle with the name of the store painted in bright orange letters, a cheerful beacon against the wet gray afternoon. It's not raining right now, but it feels as if it could start again at any moment.

"You can help me decide, right?" Charlie asks when we push through the door of the cookie shop.

"If you want my help, sure." I look around the cozy store, which is narrow but welcoming. In front of a big plate glass window is a large blue counter and stools so patrons can sit and eat cookies while watching the goings-on out on Main Street. There's a smaller counter next to a large glass case that features three shelves of different cookies, each of them as big as my palm. A menu on the wall showcases intriguing names like "Aunt Sharlene's Molasses" and "Not Your Typical Oatmeal Raisin."

The blond guy behind the counter is ringing up a woman holding a large brown box, presumably full of cookies.

"Beck?" Charlie asks when the woman leaves.

"That's me," the man says exuberantly. His light blue gaze sharpens as he eyes both of us in turn. "Oh, Charlie, right? Friends with my cousin Jack?"

"That's right, and this is Drew."

I give Beck a half-wave. He's cute, and seems a little young to have his own business, but what do I know? He waves back with a broad smile. "Hi Drew." Beck turns to Charlie. "Let me just get your choices from the back. Can I get you anything else? Water? Milk?"

Milk and cookies sound outrageously good, but this is Charlie's party.

"Milk, sure, we're here for the whole experience," Charlie says warmly. He seems so at ease, and I'm absurdly pleased to be part of his "we." Rosedale is nothing like Los Angeles, and I haven't spent any time getting to know the businesses here. Maybe it's because I haven't had anyone to explore them with.

Beck sets us up at the long counter against the window with two old-school cartons of milk. But not your generic cafeteria milk—the label touts it as being from a local organic farm. He then brings out a shiny silver half sheet tray with four oversized cookies.

"Okay, so you mentioned Brock's favorite flavors were peanut butter, chocolate, and banana. So I played around and made a few different takes on those."

"These look amazing," Charlie enthuses, and I have to agree, the four cookies each look moist and crinkly and delicious. I'm a little surprised to hear Beck mention Charlie's dead boyfriend, but Charlie doesn't seem fazed. I remember the bike ride is a memorial event, after all.

"They look almost too good to eat," I add.

Beck grins at the praise. "Voilà, we have a chocolate chocolate chip cookie with a peanut butter swirl, a plain chocolate chocolate chip, and the over-the-top banana split cookie—a banana cookie with peanut butter, peanut butter chips, and dark chocolate chips, with the added flair of rainbow sprinkles. For people with more sensitivities, the final cookie is a gluten and nut free banana chocolate chip."

He divides each cookie into fourths so we can share. There's much oohing and aahing as Charlie and I try each flavor—they're all delicious, from my point of view, even if before today I would have said hard pass to a cookie that was in any way associated with bananas.

"You have a gift," I say.

Beck puts a hand on his chest. "Thank you. The store just opened, and I feel in over my head sometimes," he says with a hint of strain, "but give me a cookie challenge and I'll drop everything for it. So, what do you think?"

"The banana chocolate chip for sure," Charlie says, looking at me for confirmation. I nod. It was tasty, and it makes sense to provide an option for people who can't do peanuts or gluten. "But I don't know about the second choice. What do you think, Drew?"

"I might have to try them all again before I can decide," I joke, and Charlie laughs lightly.

"I know, right? They're all so good. But I like the banana split. It's totally decadent but also really special, you know?"

Beck claps his hands together happily. "Oh, I was hoping you'd pick that one. We can call it Brock's Banana Split. Let me know how many you want to order for the volunteers and participants. I'll start carrying the two flavors in the store toward the end of next week. Would be sooner, but my boyfriend Donovan and I are going to the city for a few days. It's the first time I'm leaving the shop in the hands of my employees and I'm a little nervous. Not that you need to know that. TMI, Beck."

Charlie just laughs. "And I'll get you the poster for the event next week, too. It should have already been done, but there was a mess-up at the printer. I'm picking them up Monday."

"No rush," Beck says breezily. "This is my first event as an official Rosedale resident and business owner. I'm so excited."

"You're new in town?" I ask. "Me, too. Where did you move from?"

Beck tells me a long, somewhat disjointed story about law school and Boston and Hackensack that I'm not sure I completely follow. "Anyway, my boyfriend and I haven't been here very long, but we're big fans of Rosedale. Where did you move from?"

I feel like I need to take a deep breath after Beck's download, but I tell him, "Los Angeles."

"Oh cool, a Californian? I'm from Texas originally," Beck volunteers, which explains the slight inflection in his voice.

"Well, I grew up all over. My dad moved us around a lot," I say in a spectacular understatement. "But I went to college in L.A. and stayed put. Until now."

"What about you, Charlie? You live in Manhattan, right? You a native New Yorker?"

"No, I grew up in Connecticut, actually, but not near here. West Hartford. Moved to New York for college and stayed."

I glance at Charlie. I thought about him from time to time, wondered if he got into the colleges he was applying to, which one he ended up at. I could have tried to find out. But it felt pointless. I never kept in touch with the friends I made in each new town—if I made any at all. Why should he be different? "What college?" I ask. He'd been talking about NYU and Columbia, but he didn't think he had the grades. I'd told him that with his extracurriculars and SAT scores, he'd be okay.

"NYU."

"That's awesome," I say with as much enthusiasm as if the acceptance letter just came through. "UCLA," I volunteer, because that had been in my top three, too. I wonder if he'd remember that. I wonder if he remembers *me*. Maybe I should stop being a chickenshit and just tell him who I am.

"Oh cool," he says. "Like Allie."

"Yeah, we met through an alumni networking thing," I tell him.

"Who's Allie?" Beck asks.

"My sister," Charlie says.

I want more information about that, too. He never mentioned a sister when I knew him—it was just him and his mom. But it feels awkward to delve into all this history with Beck, as super nice as he seems, hovering over us. I take a sip of my milk.

"Can I get you fellows anything else?" Beck asks. "I have to start closing, but there's no rush for you to get out of here."

"I'm great," Charlie says. "Drew, how about you?"

"I might hate myself for this later, but I'm so curious about some of the cookie flavors you have. Can I get a box to go?"

"You certainly may," Beck replies with a smile. "Anything in particular catch your eye? Or I can give you the sampler pack. It comes with a little card that explains all the flavors."

"Definitely that," I say. "Thanks, Beck."

"You got it, handsome."

Charlie makes a noise. It sounds like a possessive little humph, which is strange because not only is Beck obviously a harmless flirt, there's nothing between Charlie and me. Not yet, I suppose, remembering how he very definitely left that door open in our earlier conversation.

Beck laughs. "Oh, sorry. Didn't mean anything by that."

Charlie makes another noise—like he's protesting his own overreaction—and glances at me with a sheepish expression on his face.

"Don't worry about it," I answer, feeling like I'm talking to both of them.

"I'll be right back with your cookies," Beck says, sailing behind the counter. Another customer comes in right after that, keeping him occupied.

After Charlie doesn't speak for a while, I say, "These really are amazing."

"Sorry about that just now," he says. I know what he's referring to. "I'm not a possessive jerk, I swear. I just—" He laughs lightly. "I haven't really let myself—" He stops again, swallows. "It's been hard since Brock."

"How long has it been?"

"Almost four years. Seems like forever. And like I just got the call from his mom yesterday. He collapsed at work. They called his mom since we weren't legally—uh. Anyway. I'm better." He laughs again, a little manically. "Don't I seem normal?" He frowns. "Sorry," he says again.

"Nothing to apologize for." There really isn't. My heart hurts for him, and envies him a little. I've never known the kind of love that can destroy you like that. I don't think it's possible, for me at least.

"It's just that I feel really comfortable around you for some reason...like I've known you for a lot longer than just a day." He shrugs and toys with the straw in his milk carton. "Sorry if that sounds weird. But you and Allie are close, and I know she thinks a lot of you. But still, that's strange."

"It's not strange," I say quietly. The bottom drops out of my stomach, because if I'm ever going to tell him, this is the perfect moment. "As a matter of fact, I—"

"One box of cookies for the handsome man with the equally handsome boyfriend," Beck says, interrupting us by presenting me with a large brown bakery box tied with a dark blue ribbon.

"Oh, we're not—" I start, but Charlie talks over me, "Can you add it to my order, Beck? I'll pay for everything next week."

"Super," Beck says.

I heft the box. It feels like it has way more than six cookies in it. "Thanks."

"We'll get out of your hair now," Charlie says. "But I'll see you next week."

"See you then." Beck winks at us as we dispose of our

milk cartons in the neatly labeled recycling bin by the door.

A fresh peal of thunder greets us when we emerge onto Main Street. It's early for dinner, and I'm full from the cookie tasting, but I don't want to go back home just yet. Besides, there's the thing that I really need to say because if I go much longer without saying it, my head is going to explode.

"Drink?" I propose.

"Dinner?" Charlie counters.

I look down the street and spot a stout brick building with a sign reading McGinty's Pub half a block away. "Both?" I say, pointing at the establishment.

"Lead the way."

EIGHT

CHARLIE

DREW IS fidgety as we take our seats in a leather booth inside the Irish pub. He slides the bakery box in first, then follows, and immediately grabs a sugar packet from the container on the table to fuss with.

I get it. I'm being weird. Coming on too strong. Acting possessive when I have absolutely no right or reason to.

It's just that I wasn't lying when I said I feel like I've known him for longer than a day, and this kind of connection doesn't happen to me very often. Still, I'm not going to win him over by being a total weirdo.

"I just want to say again I'm sorry if I was out of line. I'm not usually this socially inept."

"I must be rubbing off on you," he says with a self-deprecating smile.

"No—you're fine." I drink in his face and the way the low lighting in the pub makes his gray eyes seem even more ethereal, his five-o'clock shadow accentuating the hollows of his cheeks. My gut tightens with unexpected want. "You're more than fine, is the thing," I add softly. "But I can tell I'm making you uncomfortable."

"What? You aren't," he protests.

I stare at the sugar packet he's twisting into a helix. Pretty soon the paper is going to meet its limit and break.

He looks at his hands, drops the packet. "No, it's just, well, there's something I have to tell you."

Oh. This is the part where he says he's not interested. That I've ruined this before it began because I've forgotten how this is supposed to work.

Drew's eyes dart from side to side, making him look vaguely...guilty? But he doesn't follow up with words.

"Well, don't keep me hanging. What is it?"

"Welcome to McGinty's! I'm Linsey and I'll be taking care of you today." A chirpy server with curly red hair slaps two menus down in front of us. "What can I get you to drink?"

"Uh. What's on tap?" Drew asks.

"We have fourteen local brews on tap right now, including a local cider. You'll find the full menu on the back."

I roll my eyes. If I'm going to be let down, I don't want to wait until Drew can explore the beer menu. "Can you give us a minute to decide?"

"Sure thing." She disappears as quickly as she arrived.

"I think I might get the cider," Drew says, his attention on the menu.

"Dude. Seriously. I'm dying here. Just tell me you don't want to hang out with me, and we'll forget the whole thing."

He looks up at that, seemingly honestly surprised. "I don't not want to hang out with you. Why would you think that?"

"Then what do you have to tell me?" I all but growl it, my stomach a mass of anxiety.

"Okay, you're right. Enough stalling. I should have told you yesterday. I don't know why I didn't. It just wasn't—you didn't remember, and then I second-guessed myself."

"I didn't remember what? What are you talking about?"

"So you went to Hall High School, right?"

I nod slowly, though I don't remember telling him that. Maybe it came up in a conversation with Allie?

"And so did I. Actually, we were friends. Senior year. I'm Andy—well, Andrew. Drew now. We used to hang out with Paloma and Seb and watch movies? I was the dorky kid with braces and—"

"Stop talking, please." I stare at him, looking for Andy, my friend for all of three months until he disappeared overnight. He doesn't look anything like the kid I remember, but I know they're the same person. Now that I'm making the connection, I realize they have the same voice—hesitant, warm, slyly funny. The same eyes, too, light gray, dark lashes. But Drew is tall, slender, his hair's different—longer. I get why I didn't see it before, but now that I know, I can't stop seeing Andy in Drew. "You're Andy," I say slowly, my brain trying to catch up with my heart.

"Sorry for not saying anything earlier," he says, sounding miserably apologetic.

"It's okay," I murmur. Maybe I'll be mad about it later, but right now I can only try to make sense of the whiplash of my emotions over the last few hours. Finding out Drew's gay, that Allie thinks we might make a match and what that means, me acknowledging to myself that I actually might want to try with Drew—then discovering that the sense of familiarity I have around him isn't some sixth sense of attraction, but my actual subconscious recognizing him on some level. It's a lot.

"So you remember me?" he asks, as if he wasn't sure I would.

"Of course I remember you! Oh, my god." What hits me then is the fact that I thought I'd never see Andy again, that one of the best friends I ever had almost felt made-up sometimes because he seemingly fell off the face of the earth. But he's here, close enough to touch.

Now what?

I wait for the awkwardness to creep in. Now that I know who Drew is, surely my attraction to him will go away. I take a shaky breath, look at his long fingers, at the pink slash of his mouth.

Nope. Still attracted to him.

One thing at a time, I tell myself sternly. I don't need to rush anything right now.

I smile at him hesitantly. "I went away for winter break and when I got back, you were gone. I was—I was really upset about it, actually. I missed you."

"You did?" He looks astonished.

"Dude, yes, I missed you. I—" There's more, but if I tell him the more, he really will think I'm nuts, and I'll have ruined this for good. "I always wondered where you went, where you ended up. This is incredible, Andy—Drew. Sorry."

"Drew, if you don't mind. Andy was a dorky teenager. I changed my name when I got to college. Drew isn't perfect, but he's more me, I think."

"I get it." I understand wanting to leave parts of yourself behind. "I liked Andy, though, for the record," I add quietly. "And not just the name."

"Oh." He looks pleased at that.

"So you recognized me? But you didn't say anything?"

"You look exactly the same," he says. "But then you didn't recognize me, and my insecurities got the better of me. Not proud of it, but yeah. Whatever. I was also confused—I don't remember you having a sister, and Alyson didn't tell me much about you. And she called you Charles, and your last name in high school was Linden, but hers is Cross, so I'm just—what's the deal with that?"

It's a little strange to think that Drew's known who I was this whole time, and I'm just now catching up, but I get it. He didn't expect to see me, and I didn't make the connection. And Allie makes things a little complicated.

Out of the corner of my eye I see Linsey give us a once-over, but she doesn't approach. "Should we order, then I'll tell you everything?"

"Everything?" he asks with raised eyebrows.

"Everything you want to know," I return evenly.

"Sure."

I beckon to Linsey and speed read the menu in the time it takes her to get to the table.

"I'll have a cider and a burger well done with sweet potato fries," Drew says.

"Same, but make my burger medium," I add.

"You got it," she says, turning on her heel.

"All right. So tell me *everything*," he says when she's gone, with a hint of challenge in his voice.

"Allie is my half-sister. My dad is what you'd call a serial family man, I guess. He starts a new family about every five years. I was the first, then he left my mom and me, married Allie's mom, had her and her brother Kelvin, then left them and set up family number three. I have two more half-siblings who are in middle school now, I think." I glance at Drew to see what he thinks of my family's unique brand of dysfunction. His attention is focused on me, and he has a neutral expression on his face. I breathe, remind myself that my father's actions aren't mine.

"I'm not close with him at all. I barely even knew Allie when I was in high school, which is why I probably didn't mention her. But she reached out to me a few years ago, and we started texting. Eventually, we met up. She wanted to understand why our dad is the way he is. I couldn't exactly help her with that, but on the plus side, we got close. She's a great person, and an awesome sister." Drew smiles at that, nods. "Kelvin's cool, too, but he keeps to himself. I told myself when the other two get to be sixteen or so, I'm going to contact them. There's no reason the five of us have to be siloed off from each other just because our dad doesn't have staying power. Oh, and when Allie's mom and our dad divorced, Allie took her mom's last name, Cross. But I'm still Linden."

"Wow, that's quite a story," Drew says, back to fiddling with the sugar packet. "Not what I was expecting."

"Yeah. Our dad does love us, in his way, but I've been in therapy about it for even longer than I've been in therapy about Brock." I give a lopsided smile, hoping I seem proactive instead of just maladjusted.

"That's—wow." He bites his lower lip. "I just—in high school, you seemed like this kid who had everything going for him. I admired you a lot. And it turns out—"

"I'm just as fucked-up as everyone else?"

"Yeah. It's kind of reassuring. Not that I would have wished any of that on you. It's just, I always thought of you as this golden boy. But it turns out your family's as fucked-up as mine. You've been through a lot. But you're still as nice as ever. So—congrats on not letting life get you down, I guess."

"Yeah. That's one way to look at it." I glance down at the table in front of me, surprised to find our ciders there. Linsey must have deposited them while I was filling Drew in on my family saga. I take a sip, instantly refreshed by the crisp, dry taste. "This is good."

"Really good," he agrees after taking a drink.

"What do you mean your family's fucked-up? I know your dad passed away, but what's your mom up to?" I rack my brain to think of what I remember about Andy's —I mean, Drew's—parents. He always seemed to go home to an empty house.

"She died when I was little—five. I don't really remember her. After she died, we started moving a lot. Two, three times a year. It fucked with me, never staying in one place long enough to make friends, or keep them. I grew roots the instant I went to college in L.A., but the funny thing is, so did my dad. He bought the farmhouse here in Rosedale, stayed there the rest of his life. I think I resented him for finally deciding to stay put after I was out of the house. I wish I'd visited, though. He came out to L.A. fairly often, but I never made it here. Until he died. His passing was pretty sudden."

I recognize the note of grief in Drew's voice, mixed with guilt and also a little anger. I'm not a therapist, but the conflicting emotions make sense to me. Moving as often as he did as a kid would have been hard enough, but then to have your dad suddenly make a permanent home the second you were out of the house—it must have felt like a slap in the face.

But it's clear he loved his dad, no matter their issues.

"Shit. That's rough." It's all I can offer without asking if he's made time to see a professional about this stuff.

"Yeah." His eyebrows draw together to make a vee. "But we're talking about you, not me."

"Hey, I want to know everything about you, too," I say. "I can't believe it's you—I mean I can believe it, because it's obviously you, I just can't believe—I mean." I smile at him almost shyly, feeling a bit like the seventeen-year-old version of myself who was trying to figure out why he looked forward to seeing his friend Andy more than he looked forward to anything else in his day. "I'm so happy to see you again."

His mouth turns up at the corners at that. "Really?"

I nod. "Really. So tell me *everything*."

NINE
DREW

AT SOME POINT in the evening, Linsey brings our burgers and sweet potato fries, and we eat them between filling each other in on the last fifteen years of our lives. We get second pints of cider, then thirds.

By the time it's gone dark outside the pub's small high windows, I feel like I've talked more tonight than I have in the entire past year.

Charlie's open about everything and not afraid to tell the truth, even when it's ugly. He has me laughing so hard I'm begging for him to stop when he describes his first attempt to race competitively. My laughter turns to sympathetic tears when he explains how he crashed and required knee surgery, pushing professional racing out of reach for good. He amazes me over and over again with how someone who on the surface seemingly has it so good in life in reality has endured the toughest of challenges and comes out on the other side, still with a smile on his face.

"The marketing job is fine. I don't hate it," he says,

describing his nine-to-five in midtown Manhattan. "But it's a little bleak thinking I'll be doing it for the next thirty years."

"I have to say it's hard to picture you behind a desk." He's so active, seems at home in spandex and wicking tees. I struggle to place him in a suit or even a button-down shirt. But I'm sure he'd look just as good in them, if the way his arms currently fill out his plain white T-shirt is any indication.

"Yeah. Well. When competitive biking didn't work out, I decided it made just as good of a hobby, and switched gears, so to speak, to the corporate world. I still love cycling, but the pressure's off. Maybe I love it more now." He shrugs, but I know accepting that change must not have been easy.

"So tell me about college. How'd you end up an editor? It's such a cool job," he says, putting his strong chin in his hand and gazing at me like I'm the most fasci-nating person he's ever spoken to. Must be cider goggles. "And especially for you—you were so into movies. It's impressive that you actually work on them for a living."

"Hold that thought," I say, suddenly feeling like nothing I can tell him about myself will meet his expecta-tions. "I gotta use the bathroom." It's not a lie after three pints of cider and a pitcher of tap water.

"Sure." He stretches his arms over his head, biceps on display, and I trip a little getting out of the booth.

I splash some water on my face when I'm in there, to sober up both my head and my heart. Talking to Charlie has done strange things to me, making me feel like impos-sible things are possible. He responded so unexpectedly positively to my little confession about my identity—he actually seemed happy to be reunited with me. Go figure.

When I get back to the table, he's standing next to it, looking all handsome and sporty. He smiles when he sees me, and I actually think I might be blushing. "My turn," he says, moving past me in the direction of the bathroom.

Linsey just smiles when I ask her for the check. "He already took care of it. Hope to see you back here again."

The pub is much fuller now, and I'm stunned to see it's nearly nine when I check my phone. We talked for over three hours, but the time with Charlie felt like no time at all.

It occurs to me I've fallen behind on what I was supposed to get done on the film today. I take my phone off do not disturb and check my email, but no crises have come up in the last few hours. I'll just have to be extra focused tomorrow to catch up.

"Ready to go?" Charlie asks, coming up to me and standing just a hair closer than socially acceptable for friends.

My breath catches as we lock eyes. It's still surreal that he's here, my old friend. My first real crush. And he still gives me butterflies, as if I'm an adolescent again, figuring out that liking boys isn't just a phase. That this is who I am, who I want. What that means for my life, for my future. I'm off balance in a way I haven't been in years. Only Charlie can do that to me, set me rocking back on my heels, but ground me, too, with a light touch on my elbow and a concerned glance.

But just because he gives me butterflies, still—again? —doesn't mean Charlie feels the same way about me. In fact, now that he knows who I am, we're no longer flirting. When he asked me to dinner hours ago, it felt like he was testing the waters of dating territory, but now I don't know what to think.

Maybe I'm afraid to believe it could be more. Being solo is comfortable for me. Would I even know how to be part of a pair?

"Drew?" Charlie tilts his head in question.

"Yeah, let's go." We weave among the tables on our way outside. The storm has moved on, but the streets are still wet from the earlier rain. "Thanks for dinner, by the way. You didn't have to do that."

"You can get it next time," he says casually, as if next time is a foregone conclusion.

"Okay." Halfway back to my car, I snap my fingers. "Damn, I forgot the cookies in the booth."

"Hang on." Charlie turns around and sprints back to the pub, disappearing inside before I can say anything. I wait, and after a minute he's back out again, holding the bakery box aloft like a trophy.

"Thanks," I say as he jogs back, not even out of breath. "I could have gone back."

"No problem. I need the exercise."

I laugh. "Hardly. But thanks."

We make it to the car without further delay, and I steer us home.

"Okay, enough stalling," he says once we're on the road. "I heard about your dad, and a little about the house, but what about your work? Friends." A tiny pause. "Boyfriends?"

"Um, well, it's not all that interesting. I studied film

in college, got interested in editing. I liked the idea of working behind the scenes. After joining the crew of a few student films, I knew being on set wasn't for me. It's kind of boring, but also stressful. Editing can be stressful, too, if the deadlines are tight, but I like how it's a mix of technical and creative work. I did it for some friends' indie feature films, and one of those won some awards, and suddenly I was the hot new editor and had my pick of projects. The entertainment industry is not known for job security, but at this point in my career, I can count on steady work. I like it."

"Awesome. And you can do it from here in Connecticut?"

"Being in L.A. was great when I was starting out, but yeah, I don't have to be there all the time. I might have some meetings once in a while, depending on the project. I mean, I'll move back there eventually, I guess." That was always the plan, anyway. "But I just keep...not doing it."

I turn down my long driveway, headlights spot-lighting the sheen of wet leaves papering the gravel in a rainbow of green, yellow, and orange.

"Maybe you like it here enough to stay," he says.

"I guess. I mean, I do like it here. The house is comfortable, even if something always needs fixing, and the privacy is nice. I always felt like I was on top of my neighbors in L.A. Parking's a nightmare there, and the traffic—don't miss that. But I had a solid friend group, and out here I don't really know anyone." I told myself there was no point in local connections if I wasn't going to stay, which gave me an excuse not to try making friends.

"Have you tried getting to know anyone?" Charlie asks, with annoying perceptiveness.

I huff, but without heat. "That's not the point."

I pull to a stop in my usual spot, kill the engine, and unbuckle, but before I can get out of the car, he asks, "Who's in your group out there?"

"Um, there's Carmen—we went to UCLA together. She's a producer. And her wife, Bea. They live near me in Silver Lake. Nora and Mark are another couple. We all used to do board game nights until they had twin girls. Cute kids, but terrors. Then there's Gil, who's not in entertainment at all. He was a perpetual student, but he finally finished his Ph.D. and now he's looking for a permanent teaching job."

"An ex?" Charlie asks.

"No—he's single, but straight."

"Ah. Well, they sound like good folks."

"They are. I miss them." It's true, but since we all turned thirty, I've felt us drifting apart. Mark and Nora are focused on their kids and their friends with kids. It won't be long before Carmen and Bea start a family, too. Gil was a reliable friend to catch daytime movies with, but he'll meet someone, eventually.

"Well, I want to introduce you to my friend Jack and his husband, Pete. They're creative, like you. That's two friends right here in Rosedale—and they're queer, to boot."

"Rosedale seems to have its share of queer people," I say. "I really didn't consider that when I came here."

"Jack's always telling me that Rosedale is the answer to life, the universe, and everything. He used to be all about New York City—we met at the gym there. I was so surprised when he told me he'd fallen for someone and was moving to some small town in Connecticut I never heard of, even though I grew up in the state. Seriously, you'll love them. Two nicer guys you will never meet."

"Okay, okay, you don't have to sell me on Rosedale." I laugh. "I already own property here. At least for now."

He laughs too, and we finally climb out of the car. "Sorry—I guess I'm a little envious of those of you with jobs you love and houses to take care of. I like the city, too, but I'm getting a little sick of dodging open car doors and reckless people on bike shares."

"Well, you'll be free from those things for the next few weeks," I remind him.

"That's right." He looks at his watch. "I can't believe it's so late. I can't believe—it's you." He grins at me, and I grin back. "What are you doing tomorrow? I feel like we still have so much to catch up on. And I know Jack wants to get together—why don't we invite ourselves over?"

"Well, that sounds like fun," I say carefully, head spinning with all the plural nouns Charlie is using, "but I have a lot of work to catch up on."

"Jesus, I'm sorry about that. I kept you out half the day."

"Don't apologize. I had a good time." I remember the cookies and haul them out of the backseat before I lock my car. City habits die hard. "But I should probably work tomorrow."

"Then this weekend—save some time for me?"

"Okay. I will."

"Great." His smile seems as bright as the waxing

harvest moon now shining overhead. "Sleep well then, Drew."

The butterflies are back, or maybe moths, trying to beat their way out of my belly to flutter around Charlie's shining face. "Sleep well, Charlie."

That night I'm tired, but I have trouble falling asleep. Charlie Linden remembers me. He missed me. And he wants to see me again. It's like every fantasy I ever had as a lonely kid coming true.

It feels like a dream.

I try to tell myself not to get excited—that he's only here for a little while, that even if he seems to be enthusiastic about spending time with me now, it's all temporary. Cinnamon, as if sensing my thoughts are on someone besides him, kneads at my chest with unusual vigor before curling up smack dab in the middle of it. I appreciate the weight keeping me grounded. Cinnamon's real, but any fantasy of me ending up with Charlie Linden is just that—a dream I better snuff out before my heart finds itself broken.

TEN

CHARLIE

IN THE WAKE of the storm, Friday dawns clear and sunny, one of those perfect fall days that promises just the right amount of crispness in the morning before mellowing into an afternoon warm enough to go around in short sleeves.

Reluctantly, I boot up my computer over breakfast. I'm not exactly on a leave of absence from work, though I did tell my boss I'd be taking long weekends and the entire week before the bike event off. Luckily, she doesn't care if I work from home or from Mars as long as I meet my deadlines. I respond to some emails, decline several meeting requests, and check in with a few of my coworkers to make sure our projects are moving forward. It's not a particularly busy time at the office, and I don't feel an ounce of guilt over doing the minimum.

Not for the first time, I think that maybe it's time to move on from this job. I make great money, have good benefits, and the people I work with are nice enough. It's just...boring. And since I don't have a family to support, or any debt, there's nothing really keeping me there except the inertia that bogged me down after Brock died, when making decisions seemed impossible and keeping everything the way it was before he left seemed like the only way I could function.

But now I'm beginning to think about the future again. The bike race is one way I'm doing that—something active to honor him, to process his being gone, rather than just stewing alone in my sorrow. For a long time, the future was too daunting to face without Brock by my side. Now enough time has passed that reality has finally sunk in—I have to face it without him because he's not coming back.

So if I left my job, what would I do? Just get another marketing job at another big company? I think about Beck and his new business. Does he have a marketing plan for his fledgling cookie boutique? Would he want to pay for something like that?

I set aside those questions, grab my tool kit, and head out to the old sun-bleached wood frame barn on Drew's property. It's surrounded by a meadow of tall grasses dotted with goldenrod. The cavernous interior smells like the past—dusty, musty, and promising treasure buried under the rotting floorboards or hidden up in the empty hayloft. I sweep the flashlight from my phone across the mostly empty space. There is treasure here—in the form of a jumble of old tools that some collector would probably drool over, and the '80s-era Schwinn parked just inside the door. It's half covered by a new-looking tarp, and at some point in the last couple of years, Drew's dad must have put new tires on it. It just needs a little attention to be ready for a ride. I tinker for a while, testing the brakes and running through the gears. It's not a racing bike, but it's perfect to get Drew out of the house.

I'm still getting used to the idea that Drew is Andy—that Andy is Drew. Now that I know, I can't unsee the similarities. Like before, he's dry and funny and a little unsure of himself. And he's gay and cute and that sixth sense feeling about him still hasn't gone away. If anything, it's stronger now that I know he's the kid I thought about way too much after he left town.

I think I suspected I was gay as far back as middle school. All my friends were getting crushes on the girls in our class, and I just didn't see it. My mom reassured me I was a late bloomer, that there was no rush and the hormones that had seemingly affected every guy in my class overnight would come for me, eventually. Maybe I *was* a late bloomer, but when the idea of kissing went from being gross to embarrassingly fascinating, it wasn't because the girls in my class made it seem interesting. No, it was Daniel Radcliffe and Jake Gyllenhaal who started appearing in my dreams in alarming ways.

It wasn't that I wanted to want to kiss girls, but it just seemed easier to leave all of that unexamined, to not think too hard about why when I clumsily jerked off it was to thoughts of masculine hands on me. It was easier to keep pretending I was a late bloomer who didn't have crushes on anyone than admit to myself life was going to be harder for me than for my friends because I'd have to deal with this, sooner or later. It wasn't like there was anyone in my class I liked that way, anyway. I'd gone to school with most of the kids since kindergarten, and thinking about kissing any of them—girls or boys—felt as unappealing as kissing a cousin.

And then Andy came to Hall High School, and we became friends, and for the first time, there was someone in my life who I wanted to kiss. Not right away. We were friends, and then Paloma said something about how he was actually really cute, and I started noticing his hands, and his lips, and his gray eyes. One day we were watching *Clerks*, and I almost asked him if I could kiss him, but then I panicked and left in the middle of the movie with the excuse of homework. The following week was winter break and my mom took me skiing, and when I got back, Andy was gone.

Would he have let me kiss him back then?

Maybe.

Could I get him to kiss me now?

I wish I could be more certain of the answer. "Maybe" seems so high school, and we're not in high school anymore. We're grown men. I should just ask him if he's interested.

I tell myself I would if I was going to see him today. But he's working. Or is he avoiding me?

What I need is a good ride to sweat out my feelings. I eat a quick lunch, fill up my water bottles, tune up my own bike. I map out twenty miles—not a long ride, but enough to get my blood thrumming and get me out of my own head. On the way, I can stop at Jack's, as long as I'm careful to head back before it gets dark. If I have to, I can ride in the dark with my LED headlamp, but I try to avoid taking unnecessary risks on the road.

Before I head out, I give Allie a call, but she doesn't

pick up. She's probably working, too. I wonder what she'll think of her matchmaking attempt after I tell her Drew and I are old friends.

I snap on my helmet, glance at the main house as I head down the driveway. I don't see Drew, but I spot Cinnamon sunning himself in a front window and smile.

It takes me a minute to find my rhythm, but soon I'm cruising, constantly aware of the cars I'm sharing the road with, but enjoying the dappled sunlight on me as my bicycle and I, moving as one organism, eat away at the miles. Sweat blooms on my back and chest, my thighs burn as I scale a steep hill, then I rejoice in the simple, bone-deep pleasure of coasting down the other side, feeling as free as the wind that whips past my ears. The roar of speeding air blocks out everything but the sound of my own labored breath.

I love riding a bike.

An hour and a half later, I'm making a right onto Wild Rose Lane, the shady country road where Jack and Pete's lovely Cape-style house is located on a two-acre parcel of land. The trees that surround their property on three sides are adorned with leaves in various stages of green, waxy yellow, and gold. In another couple weeks there'll be red and brown in the mix, then finally the leaves will drop, making way for the icy blue skies of winter.

I pull into their U-shaped driveway and check my stats: mileage, average speed, etcetera. I find a spot to rest my bike, then take off my helmet. My hair's soaking wet. I pull off my gloves before ringing the bell.

Jack answers the door with a smile, his arms spread wide.

"You sure you want to hug me?" I ask, staying out of his reach. "I'm all sweaty."

"It's clean sweat, I'm sure," Jack says, ignoring my protests and giving me a hug, anyway. "Good to see you, man."

He settles me inside with a glass of iced tea. "Pete's in his studio, but he'll come out in a minute."

"I have the craziest story to tell you," I say, "but I'll wait for Pete, so I don't have to tell it twice."

"I'm intrigued," Jack says. "In the meantime, you can tell me how things are going with the big event."

I fill him in, thanking him again for his and Pete's more than generous early donation, which I used for seed money to get the event off the ground.

"I've finalized the route, but I have to file it with the local police, coordinate the volunteers, and get the word out with locals. The posters had to be fixed, but I'm picking them up Monday. We're almost at our fundraising goal just from business sponsors in town, like the bookstore and the coffee shop. But we've signed up almost a hundred riders who are getting pledges and sponsorships of their own, so I expect the total amount raised to be much higher."

"That's fantastic," Jack says, raising his own glass of iced tea to me in a toast. "Brock would be blown away by this. It's really cool what you're doing."

"I think it's going to be good," I say, unwilling to take credit for what feels like the minimum I could be doing. "By the way, I met your cousin yesterday. He's making two custom cookies for the event and will donate any proceeds from selling them in his shop to the cause, plus I'm ordering cookies as a thank you to the volunteers. Oh, and selling them at the event."

"Beck never does things halfway, especially when it comes to cookies," Jack says.

"Are you excited he's settled in Rosedale?"

"It's pretty terrific to have family close by. Just a matter of time before everyone I love realizes they should live here," he says lightly.

"You really ought to get the Rosedale real estate agents' association to start paying you." Pete, Jack's husband of about three months, comes into the kitchen, their chocolate brown dog, Cleo, at his heels. "Hey Charlie, good to see you."

"I'll hug you, but I'm sweaty," I warn again, but Pete's already gone in for a bear hug. He's lanky, with a few inches on me, tan, and has long brown hair that curls around his ears. Cleo sniffs my bike shoes and licks my palm when I offer it to her.

"We're just glad you're in our neck of the woods for a while," Pete says. "Everything working out at the place you're staying? We have more than one guest room, you know."

"I know, I know. But I'm here for so long that I didn't want to impose. And that's the crazy thing I have to tell you guys about. I might have mentioned that my sister, Allie, connected me with her boss, this video editor whose dad left him a big farmhouse in Rosedale. It has a guest house—that's where I'm staying. I knew her boss was named Drew, but not much else about him. Anyway,

I show up on Wednesday and there was something a little familiar about him, but I totally didn't recognize him. But he recognized me. Turns out we went to high school together—he was Andy back then—and we were like really good friends for the few months he lived in West Hartford. When he moved away, we lost touch and haven't seen each other in fifteen years."

"Oh my, that is wild," Pete says, helping himself to iced tea with a lemon twist. "So you're like old friends reconnecting after all this time?"

"I love this," Jack says, his smile stretching ear to ear. "I'm going to put it in a book someday."

"Thanks for the warning," I say dryly. I'm not sure how he'd adapt this truth-is-stranger-than-fiction tale for his middle school-aged audience, but he's a smart guy.

"There's something you aren't telling us," Pete says, perceptive as ever.

"Well, the thing is...I kind of had a crush on him back in high school."

"Ahh, crushing on the straight friend. We've all been there," Jack says philosophically.

I debate for a second if I should correct them. I could honestly use their advice, but I know I'm opening myself up to friendly ridicule. I guess I have to take the chance. "Yeah, but Drew's not straight. He's gay. And single. Apparently, Allie was trying to matchmake us by getting me to rent out his guest house."

Pete coos and Jack awws and I fight an uncharacteristic blush. "Guys, stop. This is serious."

"Seriously adorable. We need to meet this man, asap. Pete, we don't have plans this weekend, do we?"

"Nope." Pete pops the p. "All clear. You must bring him to be interrogated by two nosy married men. How about dinner tonight?"

"Drew has to work, but I'll admit, I was hoping you'd invite us over for some pool time."

Jack claps his hands together and rubs them fake-evilly. "Perfect. We'll do a late lunch-pool party thing this weekend."

"But you have to swear not to embarrass me. Or him. He's not the most social guy in the world. I don't want to scare him."

"What's his deal?"

"He's really smart, creative, interesting. But he has kind of isolated himself. He needs friends in Rosedale."

"That's easy. Between me and Pete, we know like half the people in town. Even if for some reason he doesn't hit it off with us, we can find someone to be his friend."

"Why wouldn't he like us? We're delightful," Pete says.

"Of course we are, sweetheart. But we have to accept we're not everyone's cup of tea."

"I don't have to accept that," Pete says grumpily. "I don't know that we should encourage Charlie to get with someone who doesn't like us."

"Stop it, you two. Honestly, you and Drew will probably get along so well you'll forget I'm there. He edits movies. You're an artist and a writer. I'll be the odd man out."

"What are you talking about? You went to NYU. You might dress like a meathead, but you aren't one."

"What do you mean I dress like a meathead?" I glance down at my bike shorts, bright yellow safety vest, and moisture-wicking REI T-shirt.

"You look great," Jack says quickly. "You're just very...sporty."

I let that slide, because he's not wrong. I wonder if Drew likes sporty.

"The point is, be nice to Drew. And don't scare him. I'll see if he's free for lunch and the pool tomorrow. Can I text you later?"

We chat a little bit longer about their favorite parts of their two-month-long European honeymoon, and the new Super Rupert book they're working on. I enjoy watching them interact—always in tune with each other, agreeing on most things, bantering when they have different viewpoints. They're just...at ease together. They remind me of me and Brock.

I miss being so close to someone that you can anticipate their reaction to things, and you can just relax and be yourself around them unconditionally.

While we talk, Jack and Pete put out hummus, veggies, pita bread, and dolmas they'd gotten at the market. The heavy appetizers save me from having to figure out dinner, but by the time I extricate myself, it's near dusk. Drew's is only a couple of miles away, but I still put on my strong front headlamp and set my back safety light to an intermittent flash to increase my visibility.

I'm only a hundred feet or so from the turnoff to Drew's driveway when a truck going way too fast comes up behind me. One over-the-shoulder glance tells me the driver isn't going to give me anywhere close to the three feet they're legally supposed to provide, and I don't have anywhere else to go since the shoulder is a thicket of brush. I put on a burst of speed to stay ahead of the truck, so I take the turnoff too fast.

My wheels skid out from underneath me on still-wet leaves that make the unpaved drive unexpectedly slick. I unclip from the pedals, but not fast enough, and I fall hard on my right side. My bike gloves keep my hand from getting torn up, but my right hip slams into the ground, sending a jolt of pain up my side.

Well, shit.

ELEVEN

DREW

AFTER PRYING myself off my computer at the end of an epic work day, I'm listlessly looking at my assortment of frozen meals when the doorbell rings. Cinnamon runs down the hall in the opposite direction, then peeks his head around a doorframe.

It's almost completely dark outside, but the porch light reveals Charlie standing on my front steps, his yellow vest reflecting the light's glow. His bike is propped haphazardly against the rhododendron.

"Charlie? Are you okay?"

"I wiped out at the beginning of your driveway, but I'm fine. I realized I don't have any ice packs, though, and I think my hip's going to need some ice. Do you happen to have any to spare?"

"Jesus, you hit it that hard? Come in." When Cinnamon sees who it is, he comes down to greet our visitor with a head butt to his calf.

Charlie leans down to stroke the top of Cinnamon's head, wincing a little, as he tells me about the truck and the hard turn that landed him on his ass. "My bike's fine, nothing dented except me."

"I'm glad it wasn't worse." I lead him to the kitchen, open up the freezer again. I have one of those clay cold packs and I hold it out to him. "Does this work?"

"Perfect. Thanks." He sits on a kitchen chair, unzips his vest and pulls it off, then slouches down and presses the cold pack to his side. Cinnamon leaps to the counter, as if to oversee the proceedings. "Sorry for bothering you. I know you're working."

"My eyes were going blurry from looking at the screen. I was actually just about to heat up something for dinner. Did you eat?"

"Yeah. I stayed too late at my friends' house. They fed me. By the way—" He lifts up his skintight shirt and pushes down the waistband of his shorts, presumably to inspect the damage. I get a flash of honey-colored skin, mottled red in some places, before I look away and grab a tray at random from the freezer. "—they want us to come over tomorrow for lunch and a swim. If you're free."

The denial comes, instinctively, before I can stop it. "Oh. Tomorrow? I'm not sure—"

"Please come. It'll be fun. They have a great pool, and they're super nice people. You need to meet more Rosedalers."

"Rosedalers?"

"Rosedalites?"

"Rosedalians."

He laughs. "That sounds like some kind of alien species from one of those bad sci-fi movies you made me watch in high school."

"It does, kind of. Well, maybe that's fitting. The people here are almost creepily well-adjusted. Maybe they're all pod people."

"Jack and Pete sometimes seem like really, really good-looking aliens, but they've been through their share of problems, and they're good people. You'll like them. Say you'll come."

I look at the box in my hands and realize I've taken out a package of creamed spinach. I sigh. Charlie Linden is terrible for my concentration. I managed to catch up on work today, and avoid questions from Alyson, but I'm worn out.

Still, tomorrow's Saturday. Unless there's some urgent deadline, I usually don't have a problem setting aside work on the weekend. My computer won't miss me if I spend the day out, and there may not be that many nice weekends left before the weather turns.

And it's not like Charlie's wrong—meeting new Rosedalians will be good for me. I snicker a little at the name. I won't be able to think of Rosedale residents as anything else from now on, and every time I do, I'll be reminded of Charlie Linden sitting in my kitchen, all cute and sweaty.

I hum noncommittally as I exchange the creamed spinach for butter chicken and pop it in the microwave. "How's your hip?"

"I'll live. Can I borrow this for the night?" he asks, meaning the ice pack.

"Of course. What about some antibacterial cream or a Band-Aid?"

"Nah. I'm okay."

"Really? You're not just being macho?" I walk over and frown down at his hip.

"No, really. I didn't get any scrapes or anything. Just a bruise. See?" He moves the ice pack and pulls down his shorts again, exposing a spot the size of a fist that's definitely going to bruise. He's also revealed the tantalizing crease of his pelvis, which makes me wish I hadn't asked. His shirtless torso found its way into my dreams last night, only reinforcing how long it's been since I had another man's hands on me. And there he is, right there, within touching distance.

The boy of my dreams, all grown up.

"What do you think?" he asks softly, and my gaze shifts from his hip to his face. He's watching me with an unreadable expression, but it might have something to do with...attraction? He's looking at me like he'd be only too happy to play doctor with me.

"Arnica is good for bruises. I have some." I leave the room and hope it doesn't look like I'm running away.

The arnica isn't in the downstairs bathroom, so I head upstairs to the big bathroom off my dad's room. The room still smells like him. I haven't gotten rid of anything in here yet, which is stupid, I know. I've been sleeping in the bedroom at the other end of the hall. I find the arnica in the second drawer, among expired anti-itch creams and a half-empty toothpaste tube, and head downstairs.

"Sorry about that. I found it." I put the tube on the table next to Charlie, on top of his vest so he won't forget to take it with him.

"Thanks." The microwave beeps. "Well, I've taken up too much of your time."

When I open the microwave, the scent of spices fills the air. "No, it's fine. I'm done for the day. Tell me about your day while I eat." I may not be ready to play doctor with him, but baby steps.

He tells me about his bike ride, his visit with his friends. "Oh, I worked on the bike in the barn. It honestly just needs a little chain lube." He winks at me, and I roll my eyes.

"I ordered some today," I say, a little shyly. "And a helmet. I hope it fits. I tried to read the sizing chart, but how are you supposed to know how big your head is?"

He looks at me thoughtfully. "I'd say your head is the perfect size."

Is he flirting with me? "What size is that?" I ask.

"I'm sure a standard adult size will work."

"That's another thing. How come the kids' sizes are the ones with the cool designs? What if I wanted a Godzilla or Spiderman helmet?"

"That I can't help you with. Adults are, by definition, boring. Especially bike riding adults. We're all holier than thou types, you know?"

"You adult cyclists do have something of a reputation," I say.

"Good lovers?" he says with a smirk.

I choke on my bite of butter chicken. "Yeah, that's the word on the street," I say, hoping my face isn't flaming red. I'm thirty-two. I should be able to joke about sex. It's just hard when I'm joking with Charlie Linden about sex.

"Seriously, though, it's exciting to hear you ordered

that stuff. As soon as it arrives, let me know and we'll go for a test ride."

"Oh my god, I'm already embarrassed. I'm probably going to look like a ten-year-old on his first big boy bike."

"Come on, it'll be fun."

"You talk a lot about having fun."

"Well, we're young, we have our health. Why not enjoy life?"

"You make some good points. I enjoy my job, at least."

He winces. "Don't rub it in."

"Sorry."

"It's okay. It's awesome that you like what you do. I used to, but it's gotten kind of stale. But I don't want to talk about work. We're talking about fun. About the weekend. What could I possibly say to convince you to come with me tomorrow?"

I look at him, looking at me with those melting brown eyes, and internally roll my eyes at myself. A cute boy, a *nice* cute boy, is asking me to spend Saturday with him and his friends, and I'm resisting why? Because I still feel like I'm seventeen some days? Or because I've gotten too used to my own company? I may be accustomed to being lonely, but that doesn't mean it has to be the default.

"I'm in," I say. "What should I bring?"

"Awesome. Bathing suit, a towel. I guess it would be polite to bring a six-pack of beer or something."

"That cider we had last night was really good. I could go out in the morning and pick up something like that."

"Or we can do it on the way there, together."

"All right." I flash a hesitant smile at him. I'm done

with my meal, but I don't quite want to say goodnight yet. "So, do you keep in touch with anyone from high school?"

"Yeah, of course. Paloma is going to freak out when I tell her about you. She lives in Atlanta now. I'll text her tomorrow." He takes the ice pack off, picks up the arnica, and dabs some on his side.

I try not to ogle his exposed skin like some kind of injury fetishist. "Really? You're still in touch? That's amazing. I miss her and Seb. You in touch with him, too?"

"I was one of his groomsmen at their wedding, actually."

"No shit! They got married to each other?" My cheeks stretch wide. "He always had such a thing for her, but I didn't think she liked him back."

"Well, it didn't happen right away. They went to different colleges before ending up in the same grad program. I guess they were both dating other people, but when they started hanging out again, they realized they were meant to be together."

"That's so romantic," I say, then sigh. "Stuff like that never happens to me."

"What are you talking about? What about us?" he asks, screwing the lid onto the tube of arnica.

I flick my gaze to his face. "What do you mean—what about us?"

"We just met again after fifteen years. That's pretty cool."

"Yeah, but—" I don't think I should have to point out the obvious, but Charlie seems to be waiting patiently for me to finish. "But our reconnection isn't the beginning of a grand love story like theirs. It's just a cool coincidence."

"Oh," he says quietly, turning the arnica tube around in his hands. "How do you know?"

"How do I know what?"

"That this isn't the beginning of a grand love story?" He sounds perfectly serious, but he must be joking.

"Come on, Charlie. I know better than to think I'm going to end up in some passionate love affair like in the movies, with the meet-cute and the happily ever after."

"Why shouldn't you?" he asks. "Why shouldn't I?"

"I'm not saying you shouldn't. I'm just thinking about the odds. And the odds aren't great." Especially when we're talking about me. And Charlie. Life doesn't work that way.

"Is that why you've been hiding out here for months? Because you don't like the odds? If you don't play the game, then you can't lose?"

"Something like that," I say stiffly, not loving being analyzed by him, especially with such insight. "I'm realistic."

"You're a romantic," he corrects, "who needs a reason to believe."

"Maybe. But what about you—don't you know firsthand that not all love affairs have happy endings?"

His smile disappears, and I cringe. Maybe I shouldn't have brought that up. "I'm sorry—"

"No, it's okay." He blows out a breath. "Look, I thought I had it made with Brock. Someone I loved, who loved me. Someone I could plan a future with. And it didn't work out. Just like my dream of being a professional cyclist. I've had to start over more than once in my life, and I—I don't know, it sucks. You know—you've had to start over, too."

I never thought about it exactly that way, but he's right. We both know how to adapt, to react to a change of circumstances out of our control.

"I'm not saying I have much of anything figured out," he says ruefully, "but I look at your life and I just—I don't get it."

"Get what?" I say with a hint of heat. His criticism, like his analysis, stings. This is why I don't invite people into my life—it's hard enough to be me without people judging me.

"You have a creative job, you have Cinnamon. You have this cool old house. But you seem...stuck. Stuck between here and L.A. Almost like you're afraid to make a commitment."

I gape at him for a moment, trying to figure out how to argue with him. It would be easier if he wasn't right. I have been dragging my feet on clearing out this house, on making decisions about my future.

"You're...not wrong," I say finally, with dignified reluctance. "I haven't always been this...afraid." My life in L.A. was small but fulfilling. I dated. I had friends. My career was on an upward trajectory. That's the only thing I've managed to hang on to since...since Dad died, and I came here.

Does that mean going back to L.A. is the answer, after all?

Or does it mean I'm not dealing with the real issue?

I glance around the kitchen, still filled with his dishes, his art hanging on the walls.

Charlie's watching me with sympathy-filled eyes. "Losing someone you love is hard."

Is that what this is about? Dad?

I blink away unexpected tears. Jesus, just what I need —to cry in front of the guy I like.

Charlie abruptly stands, making the chair legs scrape against the floor. He comes over, hovers near me, but doesn't touch me. "Hey, sorry if I overstepped."

"It's fine," I say, the words coming out embarrassingly thickly. I'm not crying, but it's close enough I might as well be. Great. Tears are so attractive.

"Sorry," he says again, sounding guilty. "I guess I forgot that we don't actually know each other all that well. It feels like we've known each other a long time."

I breathe carefully until I'm sure words are going to come out, not a sob. "We have, in a way. I know what you mean. I feel it, too."

He lights up at that. "You do?"

I nod, and he continues to smile at me, as if I've made his night.

"Well, I better go," he says, gathering his vest, the ice pack, and the arnica.

I both want him to stay and need him to go. I lead him to the front door, watch him stick the items into invisible pockets in his stretchy shorts, then grab his bike to walk it back to the guest house.

"You have a great life, Drew," Charlie says, looking at me over the handlebars. "You should try sharing it with someone. I'll see you tomorrow."

JACK RESPONDS with a string of overjoyed emojis when I text him that Drew is in for a swim. Paloma writes back in under sixty seconds when I text her that I ran into Andy Hersh and I'm living in his guest house for a few weeks.

> I'm at a conference, but I'm calling you
> as soon as I get home for a full report.

Drew and I agree to meet at his car at one. My goal for the afternoon is to make sure he has a good time, that he and Jack and Pete become friends, so even when I go back to New York, he'll have someone local he can call in an emergency. My second goal is not to scare him off, the way I almost did last night.

I'm pretty sure he's not indifferent to me. The way his eyes stray to me, almost like he can't help it—it's good for my ego. And my suddenly awakened libido.

But every time I make an overture or leave him an

opening, it's like one step forward, two steps back. I flirt. He tenses up, blushes, or runs away.

It's cute.

And frustrating as hell.

Then I went and got real with him, talking about his life choices and his dad as if I know what's best for him. It's clear he's got some things to work through—but it's not my place to tell him what to do.

I just can't help wanting the best for him. It's such a miracle that he's back in my life at all—I won't waste this opportunity to get to know him better. Even if it takes me the rest of autumn.

That sixth sense I have about him tells me Drew will be worth the wait. If I can keep chill and be patient, I'm convinced this could be the start of something epic.

My sister calls when I'm stuffing a beach towel in my backpack.

"Hey, you."

"Hey. What the hell is going on over in Connecticut? Drew has been all about work and I can't get you on the phone. But apparently you two know each other from another life or something?"

"Small world, huh?"

"So what's happening? I go to all this trouble to introduce you two, and it turns out you already know each other?"

"Well, we lost touch fifteen years ago. So you can give yourself all the cake and cookies and sparkles and kudos for inadvertently bringing us back together."

I can sense her rolling her eyes at me on the other end

of the phone. "Fine, I will. Well, that's cool. Isn't Drew great?"

"He is great. He's a little skittish. But I'm working on that."

"Oh you are, are you? Excellent."

"Look, it's nothing nefarious. We're getting to be friends again."

"Who said anything about nefarious? I just know you've been waiting for the right time, and person, to move forward with. And I know Drew needs someone to help pull him out of his shell."

I'd protest her meddling, except if things go the way it seems we both want them to, I'll be the direct beneficiary. "Well, I'm doing my best."

"I would have thought you two knowing each other would make things easier."

"Maybe. Maybe not." When I only knew Drew was a cute, smart video editor, I was ready to jump his bones and/or date him, whatever he would have been open to. But now Drew's more than a random guy. He's special. And I refuse to mess this up by coming on too strong. "It's just a little more complicated."

"So what was he like in high school?"

"Exactly the same," I say. It's true. "Except looks-wise. I didn't actually recognize him at first. He grew. Changed his damn name."

"Oh wow. Reinventing himself, I guess. That's cool. Wish I could do that sometimes."

"Why? You're perfect as is."

"The guy I went on that date with, Finn, decided we

should just be friends," she says, sounding glum. "Which means I can never go back to that coffee shop again, which really sucks because it's the closest one to the gym and now I'm going to have to scope out a whole new place to get my caffeine fix."

"Aw, I'm sorry, sweetie." She's twenty-three; she'll survive, but it still hurts to get rejected.

"It's okay. I'll just live vicariously through you and Drew. If you guys get married, then my boss will be my brother-in-law. Wait, would that be terrible or wonderful?"

"We're not getting married," I say, laughing. "We haven't even kissed yet."

"Yet!" She pounces on the word, and I curse myself for tacking it on.

"Never mind. I gotta go. We're going to my friend Jack's for lunch and a swim."

"Jack the writer? God, why do you have such awesome friends?"

"Because I'm awesome, that's why."

"You are awesome. And Drew is awesome. Maybe I should come visit my awesome brother and my awesome boss and make sure you guys aren't screwing things up without me."

"You know what, as much as I'd love to see you, I think we'll do okay without your help. You've done enough, really."

"Fine. But if I start getting bad reports, I'll be on the first plane out there."

"Bad reports? What would those be?"

"You know, no kissing, no dates, no hanky-panky."

"Don't you think it's a little weird that you want to know about your brother and your boss getting up to hanky-panky? I don't even know if he likes me like that." I leave that out there, pathetically hoping that maybe Drew's told her something to bolster my case.

"Trust me, I'd much rather be invested in my own hanky-panky, but since the barista flamed out, I'm back to zero prospects."

"Oh right. Well, you should go scope out a new coffee shop and find a new barista to fixate on. I have to go, for real now."

"Bye, Charles."

"Bye, Allie, love you."

"I hate that name. I love you, too."

She hangs up, and I chuckle and grab my sunscreen, then lock up and jog to the car. It's a crystal-clear fall day, low seventies. Someone's burning leaves and the air smells like a campfire.

I wait by Drew's car until five after the hour, but he doesn't appear. I head to his front door, but before I get there, he's coming out, wearing shorts and sandals and a *Jurassic Park* T-shirt. He's also put on a baseball cap, his hair curling out the sides. He has an enormous tote bag over his shoulder and an apologetic expression on his face. "Sorry. I'm here. I overslept and then I found this pimple on my chin, and I couldn't get Cinnamon to eat and then realized he got into the dry food last night, so he was full. Anyway. I'm here."

My gaze strays to his chin, where I spot a barely

discernible red dot. "It's all good. Just wanted to make sure you weren't standing me up."

"Oh. No. Of course not." His cheeks get pink. "This would have to be a date for me to stand you up."

Damn. There he goes again, pushing back at me. "Could it be a date?" I ask bluntly. Maybe we just need to move things along.

He opens the trunk and sticks the tote bag inside. I throw in my backpack. He slams the trunk shut and averts his eyes.

"It's, um. We're friends?" He says it like he's not sure, which is a little heartbreaking.

"And I still want to be your friend. That'll never change," I say. I can be friends with him while thinking he's the cutest thing since Chris Evans in glasses. Really. I've done harder things. I take a deep breath and edge out a little farther onto the slender limb that is our mutual attraction. "I think we could have something else, too. But we have to give it a shot."

"And you really want that. With me?"

"I really do."

He chews on his bottom lip, and I think it's time for me to make my case. "Look, it's a little fast. But technically, we've known each other for fifteen years, right? We're friends on fast-forward. If you tell me we should hit pause, I'll listen. But I just have this feeling about you, about us, and I want to see where we could go if we let things play out."

"You have a feeling about us? What does this feeling...feel like?"

Here goes nothing. "It feels like I want to kiss you."

"Oh."

He looks at me but says nothing else.

"Do you feel like you want to kiss me?" I prod.

He closes his eyes, nods. "Why is this so hard?" he mutters, almost too low for me to hear, and then he opens his eyes, walks around the car and into my personal space. We're almost the same exact height, but he's just a shade taller, so I tilt my chin up, hoping he's going to do what I want him to do. But I need to let him make the first move.

He doesn't let me down. He leans in, but before he presses his mouth to mine, he cups my jaw with his hand. His fingers are long and gentle, and he uses them to move me where he wants me, which is unbelievably hot. He keeps the pressure on my jaw firm, and he's close enough to me that our chests brush slightly. My skin feels extra sensitive all of a sudden, hyperaware of the fabric scraping over my nipples, the pressure of his hand on my face. I feel the beat of my own blood in the bruise on my hip. If he slid his palm a little lower, he'd be touching my neck, and I suddenly get a rush of arousal at the idea of sweet, shy Drew wrapping his hand around my throat while he takes what he wants from me.

I'm not a hugely kinky guy, but suddenly I want to see where my limits are, and where Drew's limits might be.

I swallow, and then he finally, finally kisses me, achingly soft, his lips just the right amount of wet. They catch on mine, so I open my mouth wider, inviting him in. He kisses me again, keeping control, his hand never leaving my face. I let him kiss me over and over, making a noise of approval when his tongue touches mine. It's a hell of a first kiss, more like the first twenty kisses or so, because he's not stopping, and I have no intention of putting an end to it. It feels too good. It's a little scarily intimate, but I can handle it.

I just hope he can.

I COME BACK to myself slowly. First, I register my lips on Charlie's, and I pull away sharply. Then I realize my hand is still cupping his jaw. I drop it clumsily and step back.

I kissed Charlie Linden.

It was almost a dare to show myself I could do it. I could do the thing I'd wanted to do since I was seventeen.

And I did it.

Charlie had wanted me to kiss him. Me.

And from the smile forming on his face, he liked it.

Did I like it? The second I went in for the kiss, I lost my higher brain function. I operated solely on instinct and now that my brain is working again, I'm not sure what to do.

But if I did it once, I can do it again. "Can I just—uh—" I step forward once more, leave my hands at my sides, and kiss him, this time forcing myself to stay present, to really feel the brush of our lips, to smell him, all male and warm from standing out here in the sun. He feels amazingly alive. He tastes like instant coffee.

Kissing him feels good—not awkward, like kissing a crush that turns out to be less than you hoped for, but more like wrapping yourself in a cozy blanket. A man blanket.

Okay, not a great analogy. I'm about to stop the kiss, even though he's very definitely kissing me back. His tongue is in my mouth, and the electric shock of that skitters through me all the way to my balls, which tighten, and my cock, which starts to chub up. Then he grabs my hand and puts it on his chest. I move my other hand to the back of his head, and he makes a little noise. He likes that. I push him forward, hold his head tighter against me, and his kisses get deeper, wetter. He seems to like whatever I do; however I touch him.

And suddenly this simple kiss to show myself I'm capable of getting out of my own way is escalating into something more like foreplay.

I tear my mouth from his. "Um. Are we—should we get going?"

He looks at me, his brown eyes eclipsed by his pupils. His mouth is shiny with my spit. It's hot as fuck.

"Just give me a minute." He looks down at where my hand is still resting on his chest and I yank it away, pulling my hand back from where it's still cradling his head at the same time. He darts out, grabs both my hands with his. "I like your hands on me."

"Oh." Charlie Linden likes my hands on him. My world turns upside down, then right side up again—only everything feels different.

"But yeah, we should go," he says reluctantly. "We're supposed to be socializing."

"Do we have to?" I whisper.

He chuckles darkly. "I—I mean. It'll be good for us. Besides, and I can't believe I'm saying this, but even if we are on fast-forward, I don't want to rush things too much. Right?"

"Right." That makes sense to me. And from the way he can't stop looking at my mouth, and the way he hasn't stopped holding my hands, I know he's not just looking for an excuse to stop, even if I can't quite believe he's as attracted to me as I am to him. "Fast-forward, but no rush."

"Is that shitty of me? I can text Jack and we can do it another time."

"No, no, of course not." As much as the idea of dragging him into my bed for the rest of the day? month? year? has its appeal, I am a grownup who can see that not only do we have time for that later, but that maybe we could use the space that being in the outside world together will provide.

"We should go," I say, more firmly this time.

"Should we talk about this?" he asks, letting go of my hands finally. "I mean—are you okay?"

"I'm okay. A little surprised at the way this day is going. But I'm okay. What about you?" If he says he regrets it, I'll be disappointed, but not surprised. I didn't start today thinking it would include kissing Charlie. On the contrary, after our conversation last night, I was pretty sure he would try to bail on me. I was too emotional, too defensive, and he was right when he said I have too much baggage. Okay, maybe he didn't say that, exactly, but I definitely came away from our talk feeling like I needed to find a therapist to examine some of my stuff around Dad's death. Not exactly sexy.

But Charlie, as ever, surprises me. "I'm very okay. That was—" He puts a hand over his heart, grins, and shakes his head. "Wow."

"Wow, as in good?" I'm not in that much doubt, but my ego doesn't mind clarification.

"Do you even know how hot you are?"

I blink at him, but he appears to be perfectly serious. Apparently, he finds skinny bulb-nosed nerds with pimples on their chin sexy. "No."

He laughs. "You're freaking adorable. Come on, let's go." He goes to the passenger side, and I have no choice but to get over myself, unlock the car, and get in.

JACK AND PETE live a couple of miles from me in a tidy, deceptively modest two-story house on Wild Rose Lane. Their Cape looks about the same size as my farmhouse, but it's much better taken care of, with neat landscaping and crisply painted trim. The fall leaves dotting their driveway could have been placed by a magazine stylist for a cover story on picture-perfect New England homes, whereas the ones cluttering up my driveway could charitably be called "rustic chic." I park and we grab our stuff, including the cider we stopped to buy downtown at a cute little wine shop I'd never been to before called Wine and Roses.

Before we can knock, we're greeted by a medium-sized ball of brown fluff that barrels around the side of the house, tail wagging and tongue hanging out.

"Hey, girl," Charlie says, dropping down to hold her by the collar and give her head a pat. "Where are your daddies?"

My heart, which has been going triple time since the kissing incident, melts a little. He's a cat person *and* a dog person. I always wanted a dog growing up, but moving around as much as we did, it was never an option.

"Who's this?" I ask, holding out my hand for her to sniff.

"This is—"

"Cleo!" A man bellows from somewhere to the right of the house. "Cleo!"

She barks to alert the yelling man of her location, and Charlie stands up, keeping a hand on her collar lest she try to run toward the road. Not a single car has passed while we've been here, but it makes sense he'd err on the side of caution.

We walk in the direction of the voice, taking a little path through glossy red-tinged azalea bushes, and run into a tall, tan, cute guy about our age wearing a white T-shirt, neon blue swim trunks, and Crocs. He's got longish brown hair that he pushes behind his ears when he sees us. "Oh, you got her, good. Cleo, what's gotten into you?"

He opens a side gate and Charlie goes through, releasing his hold on the dog once they're on the other side. I follow, and the tall man closes the gate behind us. We're in a large backyard consisting of a stone patio right off the back of the house, then a wide, deep lawn ringed by another fence and trees. An additional fenced-off area to the side of the lawn looks like it must be where the pool is. It's a lovely space and makes me think about the possibilities of sprucing up the backyard of the farmhouse, which has room for things like a grill and outdoor seating, but right now is mostly empty except for the weeds growing up through the brick patio.

"Hi, you must be Drew, I'm Pete Blekitny." We shake hands and he points to Cleo, who's goading Charlie into playing with her by dropping a tennis ball at his feet. "That's our baby, Cleo."

"We met," I say, smiling. "Thanks for having us. Me."

He just grins. "No problem. What a gorgeous day, right?"

"Here you are. I went to the front, but no one was there." A guy who also looks like he's in his mid-thirties comes through the house's French doors onto the patio. He's cute, too, a little shorter and stockier than Pete, with hair that's shorter and lighter, and wears a green shirt and jeans with bare feet.

"Drew, right? I'm Jack." He waves at me, and I wave back. Charlie's friends are so good-looking, it's a lucky thing I'm not feeling at all self-conscious about my own looks right now.

Oh, wait.

It takes all my willpower not to touch the pimple on my chin.

"You guys want to come in, or should I bring the food out now?"

"Eating now gets my vote," Pete says.

"Of course it does. Okay, give me a minute."

"Want a hand?" Charlie asks, throwing the ball for Cleo.

Jack narrows his eyes at Charlie. "Not your hands. They're all slobbery."

"I can help," I volunteer. Isn't that what I'm here for, to try to get to know new people?

"Thanks, man," Jack says as he holds the door open for me.

The French doors lead to a big clean kitchen, white with navy blue accents. There's a large plate of roasted vegetables, a platter of what looks like fried chicken, and a pile of fluffy yellow cornbread squares.

"I got a hankering for fried chicken, so I ordered from this place like forty-five minutes away. It's the best."

"Looks delicious."

"We'll eat on the patio, if you want to bring the stuff out to the table there. What can I get you to drink?"

"Oh, we brought some cider. Hang on." I take the plate of cornbread outside, deposit it on the large wooden outdoor dining table, then get the cider from where I left it next to my bag.

"I love this kind. Excellent, thanks," Jack says when I bring it in. "I'll have one, too."

"Great."

Between the two of us, we have lunch set up outside in a couple of minutes. A gorgeous ceramic vase filled with a lush bouquet of autumn blooms holds down the center of the table. "Are these from your garden?" I ask Jack as he pours our ciders into two pint glasses.

"No, I splurged and got Shay at the flower shop to put it together. I'd love to spent more time in the garden but potted succulents are about all I can manage at the moment."

"Well, your house is beautiful. How long have you been here?"

He tells me the story of the renovations they've done over the past couple of years. "It's way different than the little walk-up apartment I had in Harlem," he says.

You like it here, though?"

"I'm a full-blown Rosedale acolyte now. Why? Charlie said you came here from L.A. but weren't sure you were going to stay."

"I inherited this big unwieldy farmhouse from my dad. It's beautiful, and a nice little chunk of land. I could never afford anything like it in L.A., but I'm not sure I'm ready to call myself an actual transplant. I still need to go to L.A. for work from time to time."

"That's what hotels or friend's couches are for," Jack says. "There's nothing like putting down roots in a place where you can really feel at home."

"I just never imagined that would be a small town in Connecticut. Aren't small towns known for being closed-minded?"

"Rosedale is different. The locals are cool, and there's actually a decent queer community here. We even have a gay bar in the next town over."

"Really?" Apparently I've been living under a rock since Dad died. "I admit I haven't done that much exploration of the area."

"If you need any recommendations, just let me know. I heard you already hit up the cookie shop."

"Oh yeah, I met your cousin." I can see the family resemblance between him and Beck.

"Beck's new to Rosedale, too. Maybe we should have a party soon and get all the cool people together. What do you think, Charlie?"

Charlie, having apparently tired Cleo out, flops down into the chair next to me. On second thought, maybe it's the other way around and the dog tired him out.

"I think I can't plan much of anything until after the bike event."

"That's perfect—we can do it to celebrate afterward."

"Do what?" Pete asks, joining us. "Ooh cider, can I get one of those?"

"Let's have a party to celebrate the bike race," Jack says. "We can invite all our friends and that way Drew can meet more Rosedale people."

"Rosedalians," Charlie and I say at the same time.

We exchange a glance, and he smiles lazily at me, letting butterflies loose in my belly.

"Rosedalians?" Jack's forehead crinkles up. "Is that what we're called?"

"Anyway," Charlie says, "I have to focus on pulling off the bike ride, the races, organizing the volunteers, the prizes, etcetera, etcetera."

I hadn't realized there was quite so much to this bike event—no wonder he'd decided to come to Rosedale early to focus his attention on it.

"You'll pull it off," Jack says with complete certainty. "And you're going to raise a ton of money and the town's going to see a bump in tourism and they're going to beg you to put it on every year."

"Well, let's just concentrate on this year for now." Charlie sounds a little worried. "I'm going to wash my hands."

He disappears inside, leaving me with Pete and Jack, who drink their ciders and stare at me. I feel like

I'm about to be cross-examined, but they start with a fairly innocuous comment. "So, you make movies," Jack says.

"I edit movies," I clarify.

"Anything we might have seen?" Pete asks.

"Sweetheart, don't ask that," Jack says.

"Why not?"

"Well, how do you feel when you say you illustrate middle grade books and the person is like, I don't read middle grade books?"

"Well, I watch a lot of movies," Pete protests.

"It's fine," I say, jumping into the middle of their mild argument. "Um, I edited *Dessert First*, which came out last year."

"The gay rom-com about the pastry chef? Oh, I loved that," Pete says, shooting a smug expression at his husband. "You edited that? So cool."

"Thanks."

"Are you working on anything now?"

"Yeah, a horror movie this time. It's low-budget, but the script is good. Hopefully, it'll get picked up at a festival."

"Picked up?"

"For distribution."

"Oh, neat. I know nothing about this. We had a TV show made of our book series and I just stayed far away from it," Jack says.

"I was a little more involved," Pete says, "advising on the animation, since they used my illustrations as the starting point for the series. But we didn't have anything to do with turning the books into scripts."

"Is that something you'd be interested in?" I ask. "Writing a movie?"

"I've thought about it from time to time," Jack says.

Pete glances at him sharply. "Really?"

"Well, I still love writing Super Rupert, but the series has to wrap up sometime. I'd like to try different genres, maybe write a book for grownups. Maybe a screenplay, too."

"Um, if you're serious about that, I could give you some people to talk to, if you're interested."

"Really? That's so generous. Thanks, Drew."

Charlie returns and we load up plates with food. I skipped breakfast, and the fried chicken looks delectable, so I take plenty, but not as much as Pete and Charlie, who seem to be in an unofficial eating contest.

We spend lunch talking about the bike event. I get to hear more details about the route Charlie has planned for the long ride—a ten-mile loop starting and ending in downtown Rosedale—and the shorter road race that actual prizes will be awarded for.

"You two planning on entering?" Charlie asks his friends.

Jack laughs. "Not me, but Pete might." He glances at his husband over the table and gives him a sweet smile. They're so comfortable around each other, so carefree and obviously secure in their relationship. It's enviable, and more than a little inspiring, actually.

"Yeah, I need a tune-up on my bike, though. It's making this super annoying squeak."

"I told you to take it to that place in Midville, sweetheart," Jack says.

"I keep forgetting. I wish there was someplace closer," Pete grumbles. "That bike shop is okay, but it's not near anything else I regularly visit."

"I'm surprised Rosedale doesn't have a bike shop," I say. "It's got so many interesting little places I'm just now discovering. We were at this cool wine store today."

"Rosedale should totally have a bike shop," Jack says, pouncing on my idea with enthusiasm. "All we need is some knowledgeable, smart, passionate bike-oriented person to get it started." He settles his gaze significantly on Charlie. I grin as I immediately grasp what Jack's getting at, while Charlie just continues to eat a brick-sized slice of cornbread.

"Oh, definitely," Pete adds. "I wish we knew a bike nerd with business skills who could make a go of something like that."

I laugh when Charlie's expression finally morphs from oblivious to embarrassed. "Me? What? I have a job."

"Which you hate," Pete comments.

"I don't hate it," he protests. "It's just not as fulfilling as it used to be."

"And you're always talking about how city life grinds you down. Come join us in small-town paradise," Jack says, waving his arms around in invitation.

Sitting on their beautiful stone patio, eating delicious local food, a warm autumn breeze stirring the leaves on the maple trees that ring their picturesque backyard—yeah, Jack and Pete make a pretty good case for living in Rosedale full time.

But even if I privately agree with them about Charlie doing something else that he likes better than his current job, changing everything about his life is not exactly as easy as snapping his fingers.

Charlie shakes his head at the married couple. "You two are the nosiest, most meddlesome people I've met since...my sister."

I laugh. "Agreed."

Charlie turns to me in satisfaction. "Thank you! Now I'm going for a swim before you two can get any more genius ideas."

"Fine, fine." Jack waves him away. "Why don't you three get started and I'll stick the leftovers in the fridge."

"Sure you don't want help?" Pete asks.

"I'm good."

Pete takes his husband at his word and trots off after Charlie, who's already heading to the pool, leaving me alone with Jack.

"Drew—you need anything?"

I shake my head. "Lunch was delicious, thanks."

He smiles. "I'm really glad you and Charlie came over. Even if he's pretending to be mad at us. He knows we just want the best for him. And you seem good for him, so..."

I don't quite know what to say. Charlie and I haven't exactly been acting like two people who were just making out, but maybe Jack's extra perceptive.

I end up shrugging awkwardly. "Thanks."

"And even if Charlie's not around, anytime you want to hang out, just let me know."

I'm surprised at how happy Jack's simple statement makes me. It's hard to make friends as an adult—hell, it was hard for me to make friends as a kid. But Charlie has presented me with two ready-made friends, and I can't be anything but grateful.

"Sounds good, Jack."

"Now go get in the pool."

Right. The pool. I straighten my shoulders and grab my tote bag. I can do this.

FIFTEEN
CHARLIE

BY THE TIME Pete catches up to me poolside, I've stripped off my shirt, almost ready to dive in and wash away my angst.

"Hey, are you okay?" He points to the bruise on my side, peeking out of my swim trunks.

"Looks worse than it is," I say, kicking off my sandals.

"Sorry about Jack," he says as he mirrors my actions, stepping out of his Crocs and pulling off his tee.

I shake my head. "Your husband is a menace."

"I know. But I love him."

"I love him, too. He was always there for me, you know?" Jack's one of my only friends I've known before, during, and after Brock.

"I do know. Which is why you'll forgive him—us—for being nosy brats."

I sigh. "I thought when I brought Drew here, I'd be dealing with you two prying into our relationship—not my professional life."

"Oh, don't worry, we'll grill you about that later.

Especially since I can see your guy coming." Pete says, dipping a toe into the pool.

I glance through the bars of the gate. Drew's approaching at a slow trudge, almost as if he's heading to a firing squad instead of a swimming pool.

"Water's perfect," Pete says. "And Drew is totally cool."

"Really?" I don't need their approval, but it doesn't hurt.

"No, he's a huge dork," Pete says with a wide smile. "But so are we all, in our own ways."

"True." Drew is a huge dork. He was a huge dork in high school, and I liked him then. He's a huge dork now, and I like him even more. The difference being, he's a huge dork who knows how to kiss the living daylights out of a guy.

I clear my throat and put the brakes on reliving that memory. My flimsy swim trunks won't hide anything if I go too far down that road.

Pete dives in just as Drew opens the gate and lets himself onto the pool deck. His face is frozen in a kind of grimace.

"Everything okay?" I ask. For a second I worry that Jack said something to upset him, but he just sets down his bag and nods.

"I'm not a big swimmer."

"Oh, no problem," I say quickly. He's been such a good sport, coming with me and making an effort to connect with new people today. I'm not expecting him to swim laps or anything. "We're just here to cool off."

"It's not that hot out," he says dryly.

"It's a heated pool—the water's warm," Pete calls from the deep end.

"You don't have to get in if you don't want to," I say.

"Thanks." He smiles at me softly, as if he wasn't expecting me to give him an out.

"Sure. Why don't we just stick our feet in the water?" I sit down on the lip of the pool and drop my legs into the pleasantly tepid water with a light splash.

I pat the concrete beside me. "Come on," I say encouragingly. "The water is really nice."

Drew steps out of his sneakers, bends down to roll off his socks. He has long, narrow feet, toes dusted with dark hairs. His legs are pale and thin, and he keeps his T-shirt and baseball cap on when he comes to sit beside me.

"You want some sunscreen?" I ask. "Wouldn't want your beautiful skin to burn."

He makes a little grumbling noise.

"What's that?"

"I already put some on. And you don't have to rub it in that I'm ghost pale."

"Rub it in?" I'm honestly confused, then think back to my choice of words. I'd called his skin beautiful because it is. Pale, yes, but creamy smooth, his dark arm and leg hair an intriguing contrast. "No, seriously. I think you look great."

He doesn't say anything, but he puts his legs in the water, too, and moves his feet around in little swirling motions.

We watch as Pete does a slow crawl to one end of the pool, then backstrokes the other way.

"Feels good, right?" I ask.

"Yeah." He blows out a long breath. "Sorry I'm so uptight."

"It's okay. I know I've been pushing you today." I nudge his arm with mine to show him I haven't forgotten our kisses. It's honestly been hard to think about anything else ever since.

"Jack and Pete are good people. Thanks for introducing me."

"I'm really glad you like them." I feel a sense of accomplishment at having at least made a connection there, one that will benefit all parties involved.

"They're really...pretty," he says. "You belong out here with them, half-naked in the sun. I guess I'm feeling a bit out of my league."

I shift my body so I can look at him face-on. "Are you serious?"

He looks at me dejectedly. "I'm not even sure why you wanted to kiss me before."

"You are serious," I say, suddenly appalled at myself that Drew would go even a minute without knowing how attractive he is. I glance at Pete, who seems lost in his own little workout. Jack still hasn't made his way out here. It might not be the perfect setting for this confession, but I have to take the chance.

"Do you know how I figured out I was gay?" I ask.

Drew looks taken aback at the apparent change in subject. He lifts an eyebrow. "Because you wanted to have sex with men?"

"Smart-ass." I elbow him lightly in the side. "Because I had this friend who was so nice and funny and smart, and who I couldn't stop thinking about wanting to kiss. His name was Andy."

Drew's eyes widen at that. "Wait. Really?"

"Really. You were the first person I ever wanted to kiss in real life. And when I arrived at your house the other day, I thought you were really attractive, even though somehow I missed the fact that you're the same person I wanted a decade and a half ago."

"You're excused. I changed."

"But that's just it—you haven't changed, not that much. I wanted to kiss you then, and I want to kiss you now. And I think you're..." I look him up and down, struggling to find the right words. Sure, he's not a gym rat, or even conventionally handsome. But he's kind, and funny, and it's not even a "good personality/ugly body" binary because that's bullshit anyway, but I love the way he looks—from his dark mass of hair to his expressive hands to his long toes. "I think you're really sexy," I say bluntly.

Just then, Jack comes through the gate and Pete stands up in the shallow end and waves at us. "You guys coming in or what?"

"In a second," I call to Pete. "And if you don't believe me," I say in a lower tone, for Drew's ears only, "then I'll just have to show you. In private."

I figure he'll want to process that promise, so I jump in the pool and leave him to stew.

Jack dives in a minute later, and the three of us drift around the pool while we shoot the shit.

I don't stare at Drew, but I'm aware of him all the same, sitting alone, hunched over like he's protecting himself from some unseen assailant. I try to look at this situation from his point of view. Jack and Pete are traditionally good-looking guys, but Jack's a writer, not a model, even though with his face he might have gone that route. He's become a bit soft around the middle in his mid-thirties, which suits him. Pete's long and lanky, not an ounce of fat, but not overly muscled, either. I'm fit, not bulked up; exercise is my religion. There's a whole spectrum out there, and, in my opinion, Drew can hold his own.

I'm about to swim over and check in with him when he stands up and tosses his hat onto a nearby deck chair. His hair's an artful snarl of curls. He whips his shirt up and over his head quickly, as if he's afraid he'll talk himself out of it if he goes slowly. I only get a brief eyeful of flat chest and a dusting of dark hair before he's cannonballing into the deep end, coming up sputtering and laughing.

I whoop and cheer, and Pete and Jack clap. "Nice entrance, Drew," Jack says.

He treads water, his hair plastered to his head. He's beaming, and I think he looks hotter than ever.

"Thanks for joining us," Pete says.

"Thanks for inviting me," Drew returns.

And we spend the rest of the afternoon in the water, playing like little kids.

MY FACE HURTS from smiling by the time we say goodbye to Jack and Pete hours later. Or maybe it's the fact that I forgot to reapply sunscreen, and my nose and cheeks definitely feel like they got a little burned.

We get sent home with fried chicken leftovers and giant hugs from our hosts and assurances we'll see them again soon.

"And think about that business idea," Jack calls as we pull out of their driveway.

"Wow," Charlie says with grudging admiration, "he does not give up."

"Neither do you," I say.

"But come on, you had fun, right?" He gives me a puppy-dog grin and I can't deny him.

"I had fun," I agree. I'm buzzing with the adrenaline of meeting new people, swimming, eating, drinking, and Charlie telling me I'm sexy. Insinuating he'd like to prove it to me.

Telling me he wanted to kiss me back in high school.

That's the part I can't get over. The part that astonishes me beyond belief. How often does your first crush actually return your feelings? Too bad I only found about it a decade and a half later.

"I'm glad you had fun," he says. "And I'm glad you made new friends."

"Me too." We drive without talking for a while, and when we're almost home, it occurs to me we're facing a crossroads. We spent the entire afternoon together, but even though I'm used to spending days on end by myself, the last thing I want is to be alone right now.

"You want to come over for a bit?" I try to make it sound casual, as if I don't care one way or the other.

There's the barest of pauses and then Charlie says, "Yeah. I do."

Okay. It's hard to keep the smile off my face as I park next to the house.

"Should I—" Charlie starts, then stops as we gather our stuff out of the trunk. "I mean, I'm all chloriney. Should I go shower?" He seems to be feeling me out about something, and then I get it.

I'm all chloriney, too. And the main reason he'd want to shower is if he wanted to be clean in case the night turns physical. I swallow hard. "Sure. Let's shower. I mean, you go to your place and shower, and I'll shower at my place, and then we'll meet back at my place. Sound good?"

Of course, I succeeded in making that as tortuous as possible, but all Charlie says is, "Sounds good." He flashes me a smile that shows off his crooked bottom tooth before he walks to the guest house.

I tear inside, drop my stuff, quickly feed Cinnamon his dinner, even though the scamp's probably still full after his late-night adventure into the cat food bin. I bless Lucas for fixing the hot water and take the world's fastest shower. I wash my hair, even though it looks weird when it's wet because my curls flatten out over my skull, and I'm not about to get out the blow dryer. Besides, Charlie saw me wet earlier today.

Charlie. He's coming over and we're maybe going to pick up where we left off.

I put on a pair of sweats and a long-sleeved tee. My bed has relatively clean sheets, and I move some dirty clothes from the floor to a laundry basket, which I hide in a closet. I have a half-empty bottle of lube and a couple of condoms in a bedside drawer. But I'd be surprised if we get that far tonight.

How far do I even want to go?

It's all been so fast, but it's Charlie. I hadn't imagined ever seeing him again, and yet all of a sudden we're hanging out, friends again. Friends who've kissed each other. Friends who think the other is sexy.

I certainly couldn't keep my eyes off him today. He's lean but strong. He's solid, and always smiling. He glows, yes, like he's sun-kissed, skin golden and warm, chocolate eyes that could melt in the sun, light brown hair with gilded strands. But his real glow comes from inside—from his well of kindness and positivity, which I know must be hard-won after everything he's been through.

He told me I haven't changed as much as I think I have, and the same could be said for him. He's still the smiling, happy kid I knew.

Only now I know he wants me back.

My heart races when I hear the ring at the door. Charlie's standing on the other side, hair damp, in a fresh shirt and a pair of loose-fitting shorts. Sneakers without socks. His hands are in his pockets, and he looks young and hot, and he's smiling at me as if he can't wait to come inside.

I have a terrible urge to close the door in his face, to lock it and go hide in my room.

And then Charlie says, "Can I come in?"

And I say, "Yes."

And it's as simple as that to let him inside. We go to the kitchen—the only room in the house I realize he's spent any time in.

"Hungry?" I ask. I put the chicken in the fridge when I got home.

"Not super hungry," he says. "A little thirsty."

"Water-thirsty?" I'm not a big drinker. The cider the other night was more than I usually do.

"Sure." I get us both glasses of water and Charlie takes a long pull of his.

"So, do you want the tour?"

"Definitely."

We go back to the hallway that runs a straight line from the front door to the back, with doors off it leading to the ground-floor rooms. I show him the downstairs bathroom, with its outdated salmon pink tile. "This was probably someone's dream bathroom forty years ago."

"It's very...salmony," he says diplomatically.

"My dad kept this place pretty much as it was when he bought it. He just filled it up with stuff." I open the door to the downstairs bedroom, which doesn't even have a bed in it, just a folding table covered in banker's boxes, with more dusty boxes on the side. I don't even know what's in them.

"When I was growing up, and we moved all the time, he liked to get our furniture and stuff at yard sales. We'd hit a new town, and he'd scour the paper for sales. We'd leave most of it behind when we left for the next place. Once he settled here, he kept hitting up the sales. I think he started browsing those online marketplaces, too. It was his hobby. And he finally had a place to keep all the junk he found."

"That bike in the barn isn't junk," Charlie says. "And neither are the tools—some of them are rusty, but I bet you could sell them in about five minutes."

"I keep telling myself I should just call one of those junk removal companies and have them take everything away."

"Why haven't you?" he asks.

"I don't know." I close the door to that room, go further down the hallway. "This is the library, or study, I guess." It's got bookshelves, books in absolutely no particular order, and an old-fashioned pushed-out window with a window seat that looks over the garden between the house and the guest house.

"I bet this room would clean up nice," Charlie says.

It needs a fresh coat of paint and some serious dusting, but yeah, the room is attractive, and the books are in decent shape.

The next room is the one I spend the most time in. "Here's my office. I think it used to be a living room, but dad used it as his office, and I like it because there aren't any windows to cause glare." This room is the only one that looks remotely organized, which isn't saying much. The computer equipment appears somewhat out of place among the whitewashed wood-paneled walls and wainscoting.

Charlie whistles. "Your computer looks so fancy."

"Well, I need a lot of processing power."

"I bet." He winks at me, and I remember this tour is most likely a prelude to sex.

"Anyway." I take him to the last room on the other side of the hall, a mudroom/laundry room. All sorts of gardening equipment, straw hats, and more towels than a single person could use in their lifetime fill the shelves. Dad had replaced the washer and dryer not long before he died, so those gleam new, while his rubber boots still stand just inside the door.

"That's it for the ground floor. Upstairs are the master bed and bath, another bathroom, a guest room, and my bedroom."

"So, where do you relax? Watch a movie?" Charlie asks.

"You want to watch a movie?"

"Yeah, I mean, if you want. Popcorn sounds pretty good, too, if you've got some."

"I have some." Suddenly popcorn and a movie with my hot friend Charlie sounds like a brilliant idea. I think about where I watch movies and my face gets hot. "I usually watch movies in bed on my laptop. But I could set it up in the kitchen."

"And sit on those hard kitchen chairs? No, thanks.

Your room is fine," Charlie says. "And I'm not just saying that because I want to get you in bed. I mean, I do. But we can just watch the movie."

"Okay." I absorb that while returning to the kitchen. "Popcorn and a movie it is."

A few minutes later, Charlie's carrying a giant bowl of popcorn, while I've got our glasses of water. My laptop is already upstairs, but I remember something at the last minute. "Hang on." I snag the bag of gummy bears from the cupboard and stick them under my arm.

"Gummy bears, oh this night just got even better," he says.

I'm grateful to him for not pointing out I just happen to have his favorite candy on hand. "I can't believe you still eat these," I say as we climb the stairs. My room's in the front of the house, the smallest one.

"Guilty pleasure."

"Well, I guess those are allowed." I push the door open, glad I cleaned up a little. It doesn't take long to set the computer up on a raised stand I keep in here for the purpose. I tell myself it's not weird for us to settle onto my bed together. We're just a couple of six-foot-tall thirty-two-year-old men watching a movie with a giant bowl of popcorn on the bed between us, like some kind of salty chastity barrier.

"What do you want to watch?" I ask. "What do you like?"

I hear the implication in the question, but Charlie doesn't respond to the possible innuendo. "Comedies, mostly. You?"

"I watch a little bit of everything, but I guess I still

have a soft spot for B sci-fi movies." I think about what suits the mood and pull my selection up from my hard drive. "Have you ever seen *The Blob*?"

"Sounds fake, and no," he says, grabbing a handful of popcorn and shoving it in his face.

"It's a classic. Steve McQueen's first starring role. He's supposed to be a teenager, but he looks about forty."

"Steve McQueen was hot," Charlie says with his mouth full. "Sign me up."

"Yeah, he was." I hit the play button, adjust the volume. I've seen this movie dozens of times. It's a little dated, but it still has a fun mix of camp, early special effects, and moments of truly frightening horror.

We lean back into my pillows, eating popcorn and good-naturedly mocking the teenage protagonists and their oh-so-fifties cars and lingo. "Steve McQueen was twenty-seven when he filmed this movie."

"Only twenty-seven?" Charlie jokes, ripping into the package of gummy bears. "Want some?"

He holds the bag out to me and I take a few. I eat a green one first, make a face. "Are you sure these are good?"

"The red ones are the best, obviously," he says. "But I like 'em all."

I eat a red one next, and yeah, it's pretty good, sugar and food coloring dissolving pleasantly sticky sweet on my tongue. "Do they sell packs of just the red ones?"

He laughs. "Not that I know of. But you might have a million-dollar idea there."

By the time we get to the part in the movie theater, the popcorn is gone, and the bowl set on the floor out of the way. The bag of gummy bears is depleted. I glance sideways at Charlie, who seems absorbed in the movie. He jumps as the killer goo from outer space starts oozing through the movie theater vents. "This is not good," he says, eyes riveted to the screen.

"Too scary?" I ask quietly. "We can pause and take a break."

He looks over at me, his gaze dropping to my mouth, then back up to my eyes. "Okay. Sure."

I hit the space bar to pause the movie, silencing the screams of teenagers as they flee The Blob.

"This movie is a trip," he says. "You always picked fun ones in high school, too."

"Glad you're enjoying it." I look at his mouth, then with difficulty look away. "I loved watching movies with you back then. I—I was thinking about what you said today. At the pool. About wanting to kiss me back then. And I—well. You should know I wanted to kiss you, too."

"You did?" He sounds genuinely surprised.

"You were my first crush," I whisper. He's given me so much, offered me so much. I owe it to him to meet him halfway.

"I was?" A pause. "Wow. I loved watching movies with you, but half the time I wanted to lean over and just—"

Did he just move a little closer, or did I? "Yeah. Me too."

"Though we were never on a bed. Only in my fantasies. I remember your couch—I think it was some obnoxious yellow, with scratchy fabric."

"A yard sale find, no doubt." I don't actually

remember where the couch came from, but that sounds right. One of us—or both of us—has definitely swayed forward, because Charlie is close enough for me to notice a few freckles sprayed across his cheeks under his tan.

"We're not teenagers sitting on a couch now," he says, voice low.

"Nope. I remember you saying something about wanting to get me in bed. Well…"

"Mission accomplished," he says, putting his hand deliberately on my hip. It feels big and warm over my sweats. "So, you wanna mess around?"

DREW ANSWERS my question by darting in and kissing me on the mouth. Before he can pull back, I anchor him there with a hand on the back of his head, the way he'd held me in place earlier today. I burn the date in my brain—the date of Drew's and my first kiss. First kisses. Plural. Because with him, it's never just one. I can't stop, and neither can he.

We're fused at the mouth; I taste salt and sweet from our movie snack on his tongue. Our bodies get closer with every kiss. Drew swings his leg over and straddles me, but keeps space between our crotches. I drop my hands to his waist, try to pull him forward to settle his weight against me, but he resists. He's stronger than I thought. I look up at him and he pulls away, his eyes glassy, his lips wet. God, he's so fucking beautiful to me, and I'm so fucking glad we're here, now, together.

But clearly I'm moving too fast. "Sorry, sorry."

"No, it's just—maybe we should talk about how far we want to go. Tonight, I mean."

"Sure. Good. Talking. Boundaries," I babble, trying to get my head on straight. "You call the shots, okay?"

"It's just—I don't know how comfortable you are with...I mean, have you been with anyone since Brock?"

The sound of his name on Drew's lips, in Drew's bedroom, is like an ice cube dropped down the back of my shirt. I realize I haven't thought about Brock once since I knocked on Drew's door tonight. I don't feel guilty. I know he'd want me to move on. I've spent thousands of dollars on therapy coming to that exact conclusion. But it's hard to reconcile what you know intellectually to be true and what you feel.

I check in with myself. Nothing about this feels wrong. But Drew was right yesterday when he said I know not all love stories have happy endings. My heart's not the same organ it was before Brock died. It's got some dents and dings, some stitched-up parts that have scarred over, and the marks will always be there.

"It took me a while, but I've hooked up a couple times in the last year or so," I tell him. "Nothing serious. More like proving to myself I could, I think." Yeah. I wanted to make sure everything still worked, that I could feel arousal again for someone who wasn't Brock.

It all worked, but it wasn't the same, obviously.

Drew stiffens in my arms, and I realize how that sounds. "This isn't like that," I say, running my hands over him to soothe him. I never want to hurt him, even unintentionally. "This isn't just a hookup."

I look at his big gray eyes and search them for his response. "Unless that's all you want it to be," I add. "I'll be bummed, but—"

"No. I mean. I'm no good at hookups, anyway. No surprise," he says. "But if it's not a hookup, what is it? I mean, it's stupid to ask that question when we haven't even done anything yet, but it just seems like we'll both be better off if we're clear about what this is. And what we want."

"Okay. I can be clear. I want to kiss you and touch you. Make you feel good. Show you exactly how sexy I think you are. I want to spend time with you while I'm in Rosedale. Get to know you, for real. And then...we'll see." I get that starting a relationship that will become long-distance in a matter of weeks is kind of a stupid idea. But I'm not giving up Drew now.

"That all sounds good," he says softly. "I want to do those things with you, too."

"All right. So as far as tonight goes—we don't have to rush."

He bites his lip. "You said that before. Fast-forward but no rush."

I barely remember what I said by the car, still reeling from his kisses.

"But what if I want more? We're not seventeen anymore, Charlie. We don't have to stop after a few kisses."

He deliberately drops his weight onto me, pressing his groin against me. His erection, hard and unmistakable, grinds against my belly. My own cock swells in response. I groan. Fuck, it feels good to have him on top of me. It's like a switch has flipped and he's no longer deferring to me.

"I've got you in my bed," he says, rolling his hips,

sending blood to my dick so fast I gasp as my arousal ratchets up four notches. "I want to make you feel good."

I shiver. I haven't had that in so long—someone's undivided attention on me, being the object of their lust. Their care.

"Fucking hell, Drew," I say. "I'm not complaining. I'm up for anything."

"Yeah?" One last check for consent, which I gladly give.

"Yeah."

And then we're off to the races. He kisses me again, open-mouthed and sloppy in a way that makes me even harder. For all his insecurities, he's not afraid in the bedroom, taking control just like he took control of our kiss earlier today. It's a welcome surprise. I can take the lead when required. But there's nothing hotter than a guy touching me the way he wants to touch me, taking what he wants while making sure I'm having a hell of a good time in the process. Brock was good at that—he was six inches shorter than me, but he didn't have a problem telling me what to do in bed. And neither does Drew. Just another way we're surprisingly compatible.

He grinds down on me again, and I slip my hands under his shirt, pushing it up to expose his nipples. I'm in the perfect position to lean forward and wet them with my tongue. They pebble up and I suck. He makes a shocked sound; his hands leave me to take care of his shirt. Then he presses my head to his pec.

"Again," he says, so I comply, sucking hard on his nipple while he holds my head there, fucking hot. I switch to the other and he pets my head even as I can hear him panting above me. When I pull off, both his nipples are puffy and pink. His cheeks are stained pink, too, clashing with the darker red of his slight sunburn.

"You're—" he starts, but instead of finishing the thought, he kisses me again while his hands scrabble at my shirt. I help him out, getting rid of my shirt in the space between him kissing my neck and sticking his tongue in my mouth. My nipples aren't as sensitive as Drew's appear to be, but it still feels good when he plants hot, open-mouthed kisses to them and grazes them with his teeth. He works his way down my chest, inching along until his chest is pressed against my cock and his face is over my navel. He looks up at me, his finger hooked into the waistband of my shorts. It hits me how close his mouth is to my dick, and I groan involuntarily at the sheer possibility of getting sucked off by him. If his kissing is any indication, he's going to be really fucking good at it.

"Should we get more naked?" he asks, a little shyly, as if he hasn't just been turning me up to eleven.

"Definitely," I say, my voice breathy. He unfastens my shorts and pulls them down. My cock springs forward eagerly, and I hope he likes what he sees as I lift my hips so he can pull the shorts all the way off. I notice that he leaves his sweatpants on, but I forget about the imbalance when he wraps a hand around me and strokes firmly from base to crown, his long fingers gentle and assured at the same time.

"Is this okay?" he asks, stroking me again. "You feel good?"

I make an unintelligible noise and cover his hand

with mine to get him to stop stroking me. "Too good. Gonna—"

"Oh." He lets go immediately. "Sorry."

I prop myself up on my elbows, curl over and kiss the first part of him I can reach—his forehead. "Don't apologize for turning me on so fast that I think all my blood is in my lower half."

"Oh," he says again, smiling a little now. "So, what do you want? What would feel good?"

"I'm not opposed to a blow job," I say. "But I also want to get my hands on you, handsome."

He blushes again, licks his lips. "Both?"

"Both. Everything."

Then he puts his mouth around the crown of my cock and sucks and I'm in an immediate battle with myself not to come. He pulls off for a second, pushes my legs a little farther apart so he can get right in there, cups my sac while he swallows me down, and I feel him everywhere. It's been so long, and it feels so good, and the view of Drew's dark curls bouncing as he slides up and down my shaft with his pink lips stretched around it—it's better than the view of the peloton coming around the bend in the French Alps, better than the view of Paris from the top of the Eiffel Tower, better than the taste of a perfectly fried bacon, egg, and cheese sandwich, or a million bags of gummy bears.

He looks so good, and it feels so good. I squeeze my eyes shut against the mental image that springs into my head against my will—of pulling out of Drew's pretty mouth and spraying my load all over his face.

"Drew." I gasp. "Fuck. I'm gonna—coming." I switch

warnings mid-sentence because, letting go of my barely-there control, I am unleashing my load straight into Drew's throat. I try to pull out, even as I can feel more jetting out—the guy might have offered a blow job, but he didn't offer to swallow—but he holds me in place with firm hands on my waist. The one on my right side squeezes my bruise, but the slight discomfort only adds to the overall bliss of my orgasm. He milks me through the last of it, then finally lets me slip out. He reaches past me and comes back with a tissue, which he spits discreetly into before tossing, presumably in the direction of a wastebasket.

I feel spent in more ways than one—my bones are suddenly liquid as the adrenaline of being with Drew like this, and having my brains sucked out of my dick, hits me all at once. I sink into the mattress, feeling light and heavy at the same time. I close my eyes and sigh.

"Charlie?"

"Mmm?"

"You okay?" I feel the bed shift as Drew climbs up.

"I'm so okay," I drawl. If I had any extra energy, I'd be drooling. "How are you?"

"I'm hard as nails," he says. "Can I just—"

I feel him climb on top of me again, and I open my eyes, just a fraction. When I make sense of what I'm seeing through the haze of my lashes, my eyes fly all the way open. Drew's straddling me, like before, sitting on his knees, but this time his sweats are pushed down under his balls, his hand flying over his dick. His long, disproportionately thick dick, pointing insistently out from a bush of black curls. He's looking at me, lower lip curled up between his teeth, making white indentations with the force of his bite. I told him I found him sexy before, but the sight of him bringing himself off, looming over me, is the hottest thing I've seen in a very long time. It's a vision I know I'll never forget.

"Damn." I forget my lethargy and sharpen my gaze on his cock. It's big—bigger than I would have expected. I don't usually care about that; Brock was perfectly average, and we did just fine. But now I need to feel that in my mouth. I want to taste it and have it wreck me. I want to do anything Drew will let me do. I didn't think I could get hard again so soon after that brain-melting orgasm, but as I watch my own personal porno jerking off right in front of me, I think I could get there pretty damn soon.

"Come on," I urge, when Drew lets out a little gasp. "Come on, Drew. Do it."

"Do what?" he grits out.

"Fuck." My cock pulses a little at the request for me to tell him exactly what I want him to do to me. "Come on me, Drew. You got a monster of a cock, huh—bet you have a monster load in there, too. Let me see. Please," I beg, not above anything at this point. "Do it. Come on me."

The sound he makes originates from somewhere deep inside him, coinciding with the emptying of his balls and cock all over my belly in long, hot, wet spurts. He doesn't fall short—the load is just as massive as I predicted.

"Holy hell," I say, panting just as hard as if I was the one to come. "That was so fucking hot."

"Messy," Drew mumbles, as he reaches again for

more tissues to clean me with. He dabs at the mess, but it doesn't do much to remove the streaks of come from my treasure trail. Not that I give a fuck.

"Hot," I say, reaching for him, pulling him down into a kiss. "And I'm glad you, uh, took matters into your own hands, because I was so out of it from that world-class blow job. Sorry. I'll be more with-it next time."

"Yeah, no worries," he says, lying down next to me. "I...I needed that."

"Me too." With effort, I turn on my side to face him. I'm naked and half-hard, come drying on my belly. He's still wearing his sweats, pulled up now to cover his package. I yawn. I'm used to physical exercise, but between the pool and the sex—I'm beat. "I'm just going to close my eyes."

"Okay," he says. "Me too."

The next thing I know, it's morning.

EIGHTEEN
DREW

MY OWN PERSONAL ALARM CLOCK, Cinnamon, settles on the bed near my head, spurring me to consciousness. I resist coming fully awake, but brain function returns in tiny increments. It's Sunday, if I remember correctly. No morning meeting with Alyson to rush to. I have to feed the cat, do my Sunday chores, but there's no rush. My eyelids feel particularly heavy this morning, as if I subconsciously know the moment I open them I'll be vaulted into real world worries I can escape as long as I stay asleep.

"Hey, Cinnamon."

My eyes snap open like window shades at the sound of another human's voice in my ear. Charlie's voice.

Right. Charlie. Is here. In my bed. Because we had sex last night.

Completely awake now, I turn my head and there he is, all smiley and golden against my white sheets. "Oh, um, hi. Good morning," I say a bit shyly.

"Good morning." His cheeks crease as his smile widens. "Guess we passed out last night."

I glance down. We fell asleep on top of the comforter, and he's still just as naked as he was when we closed our eyes last night. By the morning light, I can see all the lovely planes of his body, his cock nestled softly in his trimmed brown pubes, the mottled bruise on his hip. His hip. Shit. I completely forgot about that last night. I reach out, touching the spot lightly. "Does this hurt?"

"Not much." He stretches his arms over his head, revealing the soft hair in his pits. "How do you feel this morning?"

"Me? I feel—" I stop. How do I feel? I came spectacularly hard last night, after tasting Charlie's come on my tongue. Then I slept for—I try to guess the time by the amount of light streaming through my window. We probably slept for at least nine hours. "I feel pretty great, actually."

His smile deepens further, which I didn't think was possible. "Good." He keeps stretching, and Cinnamon takes the chance to step his way over me and curiously sniff Charlie's torso. I belatedly realize that Charlie probably has my come on him from last night. I hastily scoop up the cat and deposit him on the floor. "I'll get your breakfast in a second."

"Breakfast?" Charlie asks hopefully.

"Uh, human breakfast might be a little less interesting. I usually make oatmeal."

"I love oatmeal," he says. "Especially with scrambled eggs. And bacon."

I laugh. "Well, I'll see what I can do."

"I'll help." He sits up, scratches his belly. "Can I use your shower? Or I guess—I mean, my place isn't that far away." He smiles crookedly.

"I'm not going to make you go all the way back to the guest house to shower. Unless you want to," I add. Maybe he'd be more comfortable doing that?

But he shakes his head. "No, yours is fine."

"Great." We just stare at each other for a second. I'm too busy marveling at his face, sleep-soft and becoming so dear, to be self-conscious about my own morning appearance. He's just looking at me and I feel...at ease. Like he's not going to find me wanting. It's strange and welcome.

Cinnamon jumps back onto the bed, strutting in between us. He meows loudly to remind me of my promise to make his breakfast. "I'll get you a towel."

A while later, Cinnamon has been fed, I'm in my sweats and long-sleeved shirt, feet shoved into the pair of ratty slippers I've had for a decade, and I've managed to get coffee going, but food is another story.

I hear Charlie before I see him, the squeaky fourth step from the bottom giving him away. He comes into the kitchen wearing his clothes from last night, but barefoot. The house is chilly this morning. I'm going to have to get the boiler serviced soon. I think about Lucas's suggestion I upgrade to the new tankless system and sigh.

"What's on your mind?" Charlie asks. "And is that coffee I smell?"

"Coffee's as far as I've gotten," I say. "And I hope you aren't cold. I can lend you a sweatshirt or something if you are. I was just thinking about needing to turn the heat on for the season."

"I'm fine. I run hot." He smiles and I huff out a laugh. "How can I help with breakfast?"

"I have eggs, but no bacon. You wanna scramble some while I do the oatmeal?"

"Sure."

We move around each other in the kitchen—me pointing out where to find a bowl and the drawer with the whisks.

"So all this stuff was here when you moved in?" he asks, holding up three different whisks.

"Yep. I told you—my dad was a yard sale addict."

"You know, if you need help going through some of this, I'd be happy to give you a hand. After Brock died, his mom asked me to pack up his apartment. It was tough, but I needed to do it, you know? And Jack came with me a couple of times, which made it more bearable."

I shift, uncomfortable at the implication that I need help, even if it's pathetically obvious that I do.

I decide to deflect. "You and Brock didn't live together?"

"No, we were getting around to it. He had a great deal on an apartment near his work, but it was too small for him, me, and my bike. We figured we had plenty of time." He sounds bitter, and I don't blame him.

"I'm sorry. You don't have to talk about it if you don't want to."

"It's okay. It's just—I thought I had it all figured out. We'd find the perfect place to move into, we'd establish our careers, we'd...we'd be *happy*." He cracks an eggshell viciously on the scrubbed wood countertop. "We were happy. And I'm still angry sometimes that I lost all of that."

"Makes sense. You had a plan, and it didn't work out." I'm suddenly painfully aware that I've been avoiding making any plans at all, scared that something's going to come along and shake my world to pieces again. Charlie's dealt with life-changing stuff over and over again, and he hasn't let it stop him.

"I'm ready to move on," he says, cracking another egg into the bowl, more gently this time. "But it still bothers me sometimes that I have to. And these last few years..."

"What?"

"You don't want to hear about this stuff. It's early on a Sunday. We should be talking about mindless stuff."

"I don't mind." I really don't, I realize. And I don't mind having him here. I hadn't exactly expected him to sleep over, but I didn't hate it. In fact, I slept better than I have in weeks. Probably the orgasm didn't hurt. But after spending the last few months completely alone, it's nice to have another body to bump into while I'm stirring the oatmeal, another person to scratch Cinnamon behind the ears. It's surprisingly comfortable. "I'm glad you're here, Charlie," I say impulsively.

I immediately wish the words back, but he doesn't make fun of me or shrink away. He looks over from where he's getting butter out of the fridge and just says, "I'm glad I'm here, too."

Well then.

Despite what I said, we do turn to more mindless topics of conversation, like when my order of chain lube (snicker) and helmet will arrive, and what's on Charlie's agenda for the week ahead.

"I have to start promoting the event around town, coordinate the final route with the police, stuff like that. It's going to be ramping up from now until the race."

On the fridge, I have a wall calendar showcasing reproductions of poster art from classic sci-fi movies. My friends Carmen and Bea sent it to me as a holiday present. We're about to switch from September (*Them!*) to October (*Forbidden Planet*) on the calendar, so I lift the page and grab a marker from a mug full of writing implements. "When's the race?"

"October 19th," Charlie says.

In big letters on the 19th, I write Charlie's Bike Race.

"Technically, it's called the Brock Harris Memorial Ride for Lyme Disease Awareness and Prevention," he says.

"I don't think that's going to fit in this little box," I deadpan.

"Yeah, it's kind of a mouthful," he says. Then he winces.

I can't pass up that opening. "So are you," I say with a waggle of my eyebrows.

He groans. "You had to go there."

"I had to. Those eggs ready?"

"Nearly. I like your stove. The one in my New York apartment is crap." He turns off the burner under the pan of eggs.

I like the big six-burner range, too, even if I'm usually mucking it up with my oatmeal misadventures. "They don't make appliances like they used to. Dad said this one was here when he bought the place."

"Want to finish the movie while we eat?"

"Charlie Linden, are you trying to get me back into bed already?"

"Is it bad if I say yes?"

"Not bad at all."

We eat our eggs and oatmeal and finish *The Blob*, and then we take advantage of our location and make out for a while. I forgot how fun just kissing is. Or maybe I haven't kissed anyone I like kissing as much as I like kissing Charlie in too long. Maybe ever.

We're both hard—I can feel Charlie's erection pressed against me—but neither of us is in a rush to do anything about it. Instead, we're content to trade lazy Sunday morning kisses as the sun gains traction against the clouds outside the window. Charlie's morning stubble feels good where it scrapes my own stubbly cheek.

His hands wander over my arms and chest. Yesterday at Jack and Pete's I felt like a wilted daisy next to a robust sunflower, but letting Charlie see me mostly naked, getting intimate with him—it's done a lot for my confidence. He wouldn't be back in my bed if he didn't want to be here.

And being touched feels incredible. I hadn't realized how much I missed it—needed it. Charlie's arrival has broken my routine in more ways than one. I honestly hadn't realized how isolated I'd made myself until he'd ridden up my driveway.

"Fuck, you're a good kisser," Charlie says, holding me at arm's length.

"I am?" I'm not used to so much praise outside the realm of work. "Thanks."

"So...what do you want?" he says. "My turn?" He looks down at my crotch, where it's pretty obvious I'm hard. "Wanna blow job?"

"I haven't showered this morning," I caution him.

"I don't care about that," he says. "Unless you want to. Or you want something else."

"What we did last night was pretty hot." I'd been so turned-on, stripping my cock had seemed to take no time at all before I was coming.

"Hell yes it was," he agrees.

"I have an idea." I reach for the lube in the drawer. I'd been too far gone last night to bother getting it out, but now I think it'll make things better.

"I already love it," he says when he sees me open the bottle of lube. "You have really good ideas."

I laugh. He's so easy. "Take off your shirt."

He obeys with such alacrity that my cock stiffens even further in response.

I put the lube aside for a second, take my shirt off, too, and unfasten his shorts, shifting them down far enough to free his erection. Then I get myself out. I warm a squirt of lube in my hand for a second, reach down and coat myself, then him. I get another glob of lube in my hand and shuffle forward. We're lying half propped up on our sides facing each other, and with our similar heights it's easy to wrap my hand around both our cocks at the same time, pressing them together, slipping and sliding them against each other, stroking them with my slicked-up hand.

It feels good, but it takes some shifting around until we find a position that really works. Charlie sucks in a breath when I swipe my thumb over the head of his cock. "Fuck yeah, you have very good ideas."

He lends a hand, reaching down between us to tug my balls, then slides a finger behind them, pressing on my perineum. I struggle to maintain my rhythm, to keep our cocks in my hold. I have to add my other hand to sustain the pressure, but it all feels good. Then Charlie kisses me and it's over—his tongue in my mouth, his finger tantalizingly close to my hole, our cocks straining against each other. I come, blowing my load unexpectedly hard. My come adds to the overall slipperiness, and I can just focus on Charlie now, focus on stroking him off. He doesn't stop kissing me, and I can feel the moment he starts coming, his entire body locking up, more wetness coating my hand.

We break apart at the same second, looking down at the mess we've made between us. Come's everywhere, and our cocks are still mostly hard. It's not a huge deal, but yeah, I'm noticeably bigger than he is. It's been an issue for a guy or two in the past who didn't like the film nerd outsizing them. Charlie's kind of a jock, but he doesn't seem to think it's a problem. On the contrary—

"Holy hell, your cock turns me on so much," he says. He touches it lightly, careful not to overstimulate me, but it feels amazing, anyway, to have his strong hand on me. He looks at me, his eyes bright. "Damn, Drew. It's going to be hard to stay focused on all the stuff I have to do this week when I'm just going to want to spend the week in bed with you."

"Really?" It's still a little too rom-com perfect to be believed.

"I told you I thought you were sexy, but now that we've actually had sex—um. Yeah. It's going to be hard keeping my hands off you."

"That's..." I'm overwhelmed, but in a good way. Charlie looks at me, the smile falling off his face when I don't finish my thought.

"Unless you don't want—"

"Stop." We've done enough dancing around each other for the past twenty-four hours. "I was going to say, that's incredible. And feel free. To put your hands on me. Except when I have to work." I have real deadlines looming, which might put a kink in the have-as-much-sex-as-possible-with-Charlie agenda item.

"Do you have to work today?"

"Nope." Editing will keep until tomorrow.

"Good." He very deliberately puts his hands on me, drags me in for a deep, long kiss.

I have no idea what this is going to become, but it's hard to care when he's touching me and we have the entire day to spend how we please. The future feels a long way away. All we have is now, anyway, right?

THE MILES slide away under my wheels, and my feet don't want to stop pedaling. My breath comes harsh, sweat on my brow drips into my eyes. I'm pushing up a hill, my thighs screaming at the steep incline, but when I get to the top, it's all worth it for the sight that spreads out before me—a quilt of color, trees of every shade of green, gold, brown, and red. It's a stereotypically perfect New England autumn view and no less beautiful for it.

I unclip from my pedals, catch my breath as I wheel my bike safely off the road. Water first, then a picture. I gulp greedily from my backup bottle. I've already gone through one. When my breathing is under control, I fish out my phone, flip the camera, and take a picture of myself, sweat and all, with that gorgeous backdrop.

I feel like a million bucks.

It's the first long ride I've been able to fit in since arriving in Rosedale, between the variable weather, preparations for the event, my actual job. And Drew.

It's a good thing Drew has a better work ethic than

me, and a serious deadline, or I would have blown off all my responsibilities this week and followed through on my threat to keep him in bed. But he's got more discipline, too, and he's kept to his schedule, saving mealtimes and late nights for me. We've gotten into a habit of having breakfast together, especially after I added bacon to his grocery order. It helps that I've been sleeping over most nights, after dinner and a movie, or half of one, followed by making out, exploring each other, what we like, what we don't. I like pretty much everything when it comes to Drew.

We're moving fast, but I don't care. Time isn't on anyone's side in this life. The bike event is now two weeks from tomorrow—and when it's over I'm expected to go back to work, go back to the life of a city dweller. It's not a lot of time to decide if what we have is going to last beyond that particular date on the calendar.

But I'm doing my best to figure it out.

I send the selfie I just took to Allie—I haven't had a chance to fill her in on the recent developments with Drew, but I'm not exactly looking forward to the third degree once she finds out how successful her shot-in-the-dark matchmaking has been so far.

While I'm at it, I send the pic to Drew, too, along with an update on where I am on my route. He'd been a little anxious when I told him I was planning a long ride today—but to be honest, it feels good to have someone to care that I come back from a ride in one piece.

Before I get back on the saddle, my phone pings with a return text from Drew. It's a picture of him at his desk, wearing his big black headphones that probably cost a fortune. I've learned this week that he doesn't stint when it comes to his gear, which matches my own tendency to overspend on bike stuff. What can I say—we're single, childless men with disposable incomes.

Nice view. And the trees look good, too.

Flirting by text. He's adorable. My stomach does a little somersault. I'm in serious crush mode. It's been so long since I had a crush. I forgot how much fun it is to tease and flirt and learn new things about each other. So far, I know Drew likes most foods, but he eats too many frozen meals, that he doesn't have any tattoos, but he's got a scar on his elbow from a car accident he was in the first month he moved to Los Angeles, and that he loves animals, but never had a pet until inheriting Cinnamon from his dad.

I haven't wanted to push, since I think I did my share of that just to get him to kiss me in the first place, but it's clear there are unresolved issues between him and his dad. It's hard to get closure from someone who's passed. I've mentioned therapy in passing once or twice, but Drew hasn't exactly responded with enthusiasm.

It's not my place to insist, not my place to tell him that he's got to face the fact that he's living in a house filled to the brim with a dead man's belongings. That he moved into the smallest bedroom just so he could leave his dad's room intact. That he's been living in Rosedale for months without officially changing his residence.

Those would be subjects a boyfriend might bring up. And I'm not Drew's boyfriend. Not yet.

Though I hope that if things keep going the way they've been going, I'll earn that title before much longer.

I text him back, adjust my helmet, get back on my bike. I've got eighteen miles to cover before I'm back in Rosedale, and it's downhill most of the way.

LATER, I detour to Rosedale's accurately named Main Street, whose blocks of cute stores include coffee shop Hot Brew, Beck's Cookie Counter, and the Irish pub where Drew told me who he really was. The street is too narrow for a dedicated bike lane, so I carefully take up space in the regular lane. None of the cars are going very fast, so I can cruise slowly, pleased to see a number of posters for the bike event up in store windows. Registrations close this weekend, and we're almost at full capacity. I'm hoping that after the riders' pledges are tallied up, we'll handily beat my target fundraising goal.

I'm trying to decide if I need to stop at Beck's for a cookie—or four—when I see a young woman kneeling next to a bike on the sidewalk in front of the bookshop. She's fiddling with the chain. I hop off my bike and walk it over to her.

"Want a hand?"

She looks up, fire in her dark brown eyes. "I'm about to murder this chain. It's been coming off all week."

"I can look at it if you'd like," I offer, my tone light. I don't want to pressure her—maybe she's got this. Nothing more annoying than a bike bro trying to help when you don't actually need it.

"That would be great, thanks," she says. "My car's in

the shop, so I've been biking to work, but clearly something's wrong."

I find a spot to leave my bike for a minute, take off my helmet. "You work in the bookshop?" I've been in a couple of times to talk to the owner—Trish, I think her name is.

"Yeah, I'm Melissa," she says. "I'd offer you a hand, but I'm all greasy." She looks down at her right hand with distaste. There's definitely black grease all over it.

"Charlie, and I get it." I pull a wipe from my saddlebag and hand it to her, then bend down to look at her chain. "I think it needs to be tightened. I don't have the tools to do it here, but I can put it back on for you and you should be able to ride home. Then you should get it taken care of. The nearest bike shop's in Midville."

"Thanks. Good to know. Is it something I could do myself? I know nothing about mechanical things, but I'm a DIY kind of girl. My girlfriend could help me, too. She's much more mechanically minded than I am. She rebuilt Hot Brew's espresso machine herself last year when the technicians were going to take a week to get out there."

"You could probably figure it out from some YouTube videos." I take my gloves off so they don't get greasy when I thread the chain back onto her gears, then use a wipe to clean up. "You're good temporarily."

"Thanks, Charlie." Melissa smiles at me. "Next time you come into the bookshop, I'll give you the employee discount."

"Not necessary," I say, waving away the offer. "We bikers gotta stick together."

She laughs, then cocks her head at me. "Wait—you're the one organizing the bike race that's coming up, right?"

"That's me."

"Oh cool, I was thinking about signing up. You don't have to be, like, a professional, or anything?"

"Definitely not. You should totally sign up."

"It sounds fun, plus I love the cause. My aunt struggled to get over Lyme disease last year. It can be really disruptive if you don't catch it early."

"Absolutely. I'm sorry she had to deal with that. Lyme disease infections have been on the rise for years. Anything we can do to raise awareness is worth it."

"Well, thanks for your help with the bike. I'll see you soon, I hope."

Melissa puts on her cool roller-derby-style helmet and rides toward the coffee shop, where she waves through the window before cycling on.

Rosedale is so freaking charming.

I decide to reward my virtuousness with a cookie, and bring a couple home to Drew, too, for bonus points. I park my bike outside Beck's Cookie Counter. I don't have a bike lock on me, but I'm betting it's pretty safe, plus I can keep an eye on it through the window. Beck's working, so I give him a warm greeting, which he returns.

"Charlie! Did you ride your bike here? That's so cool. I don't have a bike. I should totally get a bike! Where do you get a bike?"

Beck is like his cousin Jack, only speeded-up. I like him. "You should one hundred percent get a bike. And you could order one online or go to a sporting goods store.

I can give you some suggestions of what kind of bike might be a good fit for you."

"There are different kinds of bikes?"

"Sure, I've got a typical road bike, but you might want a hybrid, something with slightly wider tires, or a comfort bike just for riding around town. Then there are mountain bikes, gravel bikes—"

He stops me with a hand on my arm. "I know who to call when I'm ready to dive in. Thanks, Charlie."

I smile. "I get carried away with this stuff sometimes."

"It's cool—you love it. I'm the same way about cookies. Speaking of—what can I get you?"

I order a healthy-ish oatmeal raisin cookie and get a Brock's Banana Split cookie to take home to Drew. "Actually, make that two."

"They've been selling well," Beck says as he rings me up. "I love the idea of supporting a good cause with my cookies—maybe I'll do a different special cookie each quarter or something to benefit a different nonprofit."

"That would be a great marketing hook."

"That's what you do, right? Marketing?" Beck hands me a small box with my cookies. "I have been so busy with physically getting the shop open and figuring out how to produce all the cookies every day, I haven't even set up a website yet. But I kind of dove into this business owner thing headfirst."

"Well, it seems like you're off to a good start."

"I don't suppose you'd let me buy you lunch and get your take on some marketing stuff, would you?"

"Anytime."

It's getting late, and after my bike ride I want to take a

hot shower, wrest Drew away from his computer, and cuddle up in bed with takeout and cookies for dessert. Other things for dessert, too, if I'm lucky.

I say goodbye to Beck, stash the cookies in my saddlebag, and get back on my bike. On the way home, I think about Rosedale, about how I've had more interpersonal interactions here in a week than the last three months in the city. I used to like New York more—the bustle, the food, the nightlife. But now, I don't know. Maybe I'm getting older and have less energy for carving out a small space in a gigantic pond.

Rosedale is a small pond where I could make more of a difference.

And yeah, maybe the town could use a bike shop where people could get tune-ups and buy parts, even get a bike. I get an image in my head of a little kid coming in and picking out their very first bike. Helping them choose the right one might turn them into a lifelong cyclist.

I shake my head to clear the vision. Just because Rosedale needs a bike shop doesn't mean I'm the right person to make it happen. I know nothing about opening and running a business. Except—that's a lie. My mom's a business owner. She's had a hair salon in West Hartford for thirty years. Plus, I'm a marketing expert—and a good part of what makes a small business successful is marketing. I know how to work on bikes, and I could probably hire someone else to do that part if I needed to.

Maybe it's not such a wild idea after all.

On the other hand, I think I've got enough on my plate at the moment.

Like talking my crush into bed.

TWENTY

DREW

I LOOK at the clock for the third time in half an hour. Charlie still isn't home, and the closer it gets to dark, the more trouble I have focusing on the tweaks I'm making to a scene. He set out for a long ride today, and I suddenly realized how vulnerable he is. Nothing but his helmet and his road savvy to protect him from cars and trucks and distracted drivers and flat-out careless people.

I trust him to make smart decisions, trust that he's ridden enough on busy roads to know how to avoid bad situations, as much as anyone can. But something could still happen, and I'll feel better when he's safe and sound where I can see him. Touch him. Kiss him.

A notification flashes across my screen, but it's not from the right sibling. Alyson was out yesterday for jury duty, and she started late today due to a dentist appointment.

> I have some questions about what
> Phoebe says she wants for scene 34.
> Chat?

> Yep. I'll get in the room.

So far, I've been keeping things focused on work with Alyson and avoiding most of her probing questions. I figured it was more Charlie's responsibility to fill his sister in on what's been going on with us.

When we talked about it, he said he'd tell her that we were "exploring our friendship." I rolled my eyes and asked if that was what the hip young gays were calling it now? He laughed, and we sort of forgot to finish the conversation because we were too busy "exploring."

I enter our video chat and Alyson pops up a second later.

"Hey Drew, just a couple questions."

"Sure. How was your dentist appointment?"

She gives me a look. "Oh, now you want to talk personal stuff?"

I wince. "Sorry. It's been kind of awkward."

"It's fine. I get it. Sorry. You're my boss and I brought this on myself," she says, showing more insight than I would have given her credit for. And then she goes and ruins it with, "Oh my lord, is that a *hickey* on your neck?"

I blush and tug the collar of my shirt higher on the left side, because there is, in fact, a hickey at the base of my neck. A small, barely there hickey, but a hickey nonetheless. Charlie gave it to me last night when I was giving him a prostate massage. He really liked it, I think. So much so that he sucked a hickey onto my neck while he was coming.

But I can't tell his sister that. "Uh. Sorry about that—"

"Don't apologize," she interrupts, a smile growing on her face. "Do you know how fantastic this is?"

Well, the sex has been pretty fantastic, in my opinion, but again, not telling his sister that. "Is it?" I say mildly, because no matter what's happening with Charlie, I am still her boss.

"I'm just so, so happy that Charlie's trying again. It's been really hard for him. And you're just what he needed! And I'm just as happy that you're interacting with another human being on a regular basis. I'm—ahhh! —so proud of both of you."

I decide to embrace her enthusiasm rather than be offended by her undiplomatic words.

"Uh. Thanks. Well, your brother is a great guy," I say, because that seems safe. And true.

"He is a great guy. You know, he's the only one in my family who cares about me. I mean, my mom's fine, but she's busy with my brother. He still lives at home. Charlie came to my college graduation. He never forgets a birthday. Hell, he sends me presents on National Siblings Day, or whatever made-up bullshit holiday it is."

It doesn't surprise me that Charlie's that thoughtful. "Did you know Brock?" I ask, since my no talking about non-work stuff rule is out the window.

"I never met him. I only really started talking to Charlie a little bit after Brock died. Maybe that's why we got close as fast as we did. I was hurting, at college and lonely, and fixating on the way my dad seemed to entirely forget about me after he left. Charlie was hurting, too. He really loved Brock." She looks away from the camera, then back at me. I'm struck by how young she is—almost a whole decade younger than me and Charlie—and by her compassion. Something she shares with her brother. Her face brightens, and she says, "But he has you now!" As if that makes up for everything.

I shake my head. Maybe she's too young to under-stand that having a boyfriend—and we haven't even called what we're doing that—isn't a golden ticket to happiness.

"Look, Alyson, I'm happy Charlie and I reconnected, and I'm loving spending time with him, but I don't want you to think this is something it isn't."

"What do you mean?"

"Just that—look, it's early. I don't know what's going to happen, and I don't think it's a good idea to get ahead of ourselves." He and I have suddenly lost touch before. I don't honestly think that Charlie would just disappear one day, like my childhood vanishing acts. But I guess I've had too much experience having the ground ripped out from under me to feel anywhere near comfortable. We've only been doing...whatever this is...for a week.

"Don't you like him?" Alyson asks, a hint of whini-ness in her voice.

"Of course I do." This past week has been one of the best of my life. What's not to like about a hot guy wanting to spend every spare minute with me, cooking breakfast together in the mornings, stealing lunch hours in the kitchen with Cinnamon winding around our ankles, watching movies as foreplay?

It's been fast, but not artificial. We're getting to know each other, rubbing against each other, each new thing we learn and each new facet we reveal, carving out another microscopic layer of intimacy. He's been creating a new Charlie-shaped space in my life. Maybe there's no such thing as a perfect fit right away, but the more we discover about each other, the smoother the edges get and the more it feels like he's been part of my life all along. And like if he ever left, he'd leave a hole that would be hard to fill back up again.

But as natural as it's been, that doesn't mean we have everything figured out. And I couldn't explain all of this to Alyson, even if it was my place to do so.

"Look, it's complicated. I know you care about both of us, and I care about both of you. But I think you need to let us navigate this on our own." Hopefully that sounds professional and adult. "Now, what questions did you have about scene 34?"

She takes a moment to respond. "I'll be good, I swear. Just know that I'm rooting for you guys, okay?"

"Thanks." We talk about work; our deadline to deliver the rough cut is creeping up surprisingly fast, but even with the unexpected distraction of Charlie, we've stayed on schedule.

"I'll see you Monday," she says when we're about to sign off. "Have a great weekend!"

I don't hear any innuendo in her voice, and I'm grateful. I'm doubly grateful when I get a text from Charlie that he's back and he'll be over after he showers and what do I think of takeout Italian for dinner?

Italian's perfect. See you soon.

I save my work, respond to a couple of emails, then shut down my computer for the weekend. It feels good to log off, to have a reason to.

Charlie still rings the bell when he comes over, which I find charming, like I'm being wooed by the boy next door. The box of cookies he brings me is better than flowers. And the kiss he plants on me when he gets inside is better than anything.

"So Italian? There's that place on Main Street. I think they deliver if you order over a certain amount."

"Someone's hungry."

"I rode almost sixty miles today. I'm starving." He kisses me again, nips at my bottom lip.

I laugh. "Seems like you aren't just hungry for carbs."

"I am a man of many appetites."

"Oh, that reminds me." I bring him to my office where I brought the package that was delivered earlier. "My helmet came," I say, pulling the dark blue dome out of the box. "And so did the chain lube." I pull that out and present it to him with a flourish. "And also regular lube." I pull another bottle out of the box. "Thought I better stock up."

"I'll say it again—you have the best ideas," he says, kissing me. "This is great. We can get you on the bike tomorrow. It's supposed to be a beautiful day."

"Oh. So soon?" I knew that was the whole point of

me getting these things, but I somehow shoved the concept of actually riding a bike to the back of my brain.

"Come on, it'll be fun. Trust me. Now let's order before I eat you." He lightly bites my earlobe, and I yelp, surprisingly aroused at the idea of Charlie making a meal of me.

THE NEXT MORNING dawns as beautiful as Charlie promised, or at least I assume it was beautiful at dawn. We slept in far later than usual—or I should say, Cinnamon allowed us to sleep in far later than usual.

Last night over our pasta and salads, I got to hear about Charlie's adventures in Rosedale. After he told me about coming to a woman's rescue by putting the chain back on her bike, I commented mildly that it did seem as if the town could use a local bike shop.

He didn't respond, and I didn't push. I'm in no position to give anyone life advice, and I'm not about to encourage him to quit his job and open a business here, even if it would give me a massive incentive to finally decide to stay.

We moved off the subject and onto the cookies he'd brought for dessert. Then we tested out the bottle of lube —it was deemed satisfactory—while we made out and jerked off together, eventually falling asleep with him as the big spoon, Cinnamon curled up in the comma of our bodies.

After breakfast, I try luring Charlie back to bed with the bribe of a blow job, but he's having none of it.

"Come on, let's just get the bike adjusted for you. Then we'll see, okay?"

That doesn't seem too daunting, so I follow him out to the barn. It's a clear day, but there's a definite chill in the air, and I'm glad I'm wearing layers. Charlie's in only his athletic shorts and a T-shirt, but he seems comfortable.

"Here we go," he says, wheeling the bike out of the barn and onto the little gravel patch outside the open barn door. He's brought a pair of rubber gloves and a wad of paper towels, and he dons the gloves to demonstrate how to drop the lube in a steady stream over the chain while the paper towels catch the drips.

"You move the pedals so we can cycle through the entire chain, okay?"

I do what I'm told, and pretty soon we have a newly lubed chain. It's not so challenging an endeavor when I have Charlie by my side calmly explaining how everything works. He helps me adjust the seat for my height, fiddles a little with the brakes. "You're all set. Helmet on." I put it on, and he adjusts the straps. It's a little overwhelming having Charlie right there, his brown eyes focused intently on his task, his gold-tipped lashes infinitely distracting.

"You should be good. How does that feel?" he asks, tugging on the helmet's nylon strap one last time to make sure it's nice and snug, the snap hanging just below my chin.

I can't resist stealing a brief kiss. "Feels great."

He smiles, as if pleased with my daring. "Okay— you're ready."

"Aren't you going to ride, too?"

"Let's get you comfortable first."

"All right." My heart's beating fast as I grab the handlebars, put one foot on the pedal, push off, and then —I'm riding. The half-gravel, half-grass area in front of the barn is a bit of a bumpy ride, but I'm not wobbling, just smoothly moving the pedals and propelling myself forward.

"Looking good," Charlie calls. "Try turning back."

I'm nearly out of room as I head toward some bushes and undergrowth, but I make a wide arc and ride back the way I came. I aim for Charlie, who looks delighted with my progress, until suddenly I get too close.

"Squeeze the right brake," he says quickly, stepping out of the way before I run him over.

I hit the brake hard and the bike jerks to a stop. I manage to get a foot on the ground before I fall over, but it's a near thing.

"Okay, so we'll work on stopping. Otherwise, you're doing great."

"That was...surprisingly fun," I say.

"Yes!" He pumps his fist. "We should practice some more on your property before going on the road. It's different when you're sharing space with cars. You have to be able to think fast."

"Okay, I'm good to work my way up to that."

"Let me go grab my bike and we can go to the end of the driveway and back."

"Sure." Suddenly, I feel like an idiot. This is baby stuff for him. "Do you really want to? I can practice on my own if you want to go on a real ride."

"Are you kidding? This is exactly what I want to be doing today. Give me a minute, okay?"

I watch him jog in the direction of the guest house and try to believe him.

TWENTY-ONE
DREW

AN HOUR LATER, we've gone up and down the driveway three times, and I've definitely built up my confidence. It's a nice bike, nothing fancy, but it fits me. My dad and I were about the same height, after all. I try to picture him riding it and fail—he wasn't the most athletic guy in the world. Not that I am, either, but I used to jog occasionally in L.A., or hike one of the canyons with a friend. Still, I'm out of breath after our practice.

"Tomorrow we should ride downtown. On a Sunday, there won't be as much traffic and we can take our time. We can even follow the route I have planned out for the event races. It's less than a mile—and we don't have to go fast, obviously."

"You don't have to convince me. I need the practice, and I'd rather do it with you than by myself." Spending another Sunday with Charlie? I'd sign up for worse than cruising around Rosedale by bike.

"Cool. Well, we better stop before you get sick of it and never want to get on a bike again."

I appreciate him not wanting to burn me out, but so far, this has been way more fun than I expected. "Where do you think I should keep it?"

"How about the back patio—if there's a place where it'll be out of any rain."

He leaves his bike out front, and we walk mine to the back of the house and find the perfect spot. It's cool that this old bike is getting a second, or maybe third, life, thanks to Charlie. I unbuckle my helmet and run a hand through my surprisingly sweaty hair. "I need a shower."

Charlie takes the helmet out of my hands, drapes it over the handlebars, then pushes me back against the side of the house, under the shade of the eave. He nuzzles my neck, then licks a stripe up the side. "You're perfect the way you are."

"So exercise turns you on?" Makes sense, him being such an active guy.

"Apparently exercise with you does," he says, kissing his way across my jaw, finding my mouth and staying there. Eventually, he pulls away to say, "Can you blame me—you're so long and lean and you look good on a bike."

"Is this bike riding thing some kind of kink?" I tease.

"Just a bonus," he says, kissing me again, his hands sneaking under my shirt and rubbing over my nipples. He knows how sensitive they are, how playing with them turns me into a needy mess, and he uses that knowledge to his advantage now, scraping his nails over them until I'm hissing and arching into him.

He plucks at them, still kissing me, until I'm so desperate I push him away and flip him around so he's the one against the house and I'm grinding into him ruthlessly hard, literally growling as I take control. The satisfied grin on his face when I check in leads me to believe this is the outcome he was hoping for. I kiss the smile off his face, shove my tongue down his throat. I capture his arms and press them hard against the wall. "Stay," I say, then I release him, trusting him to do what I tell him.

I push his shirt up, nosing along his sternum. He's warm and a little sweaty, too, and I inhale him, all fresh and male. I lick his nipples, then blow on the wet spots until he shivers. Somewhere in the back of my mind, I'm a little surprised that we're doing this outside. Not that I have neighbors to scandalize, or anyone who's going to stop by and stumble upon us, but it's still not exactly my usual thing.

The faded early October sun is warm on my back, and Charlie looks good and smells good, and I want him in a way I've never wanted anyone else.

Dropping to my knees, I pull down his shorts and boxer briefs in one move, then look up at him. His entire body is taut, like he's fighting himself to keep his arms where I put them instead of carding them through my hair.

"Good," I say. "Stay." There's nothing left in me for more than one-syllable words, but he gets the picture and obeys. Then I suck his balls into my mouth, getting them nice and wet in turn, before I train my attention on his dick, bobbing hopefully in front of my face. I suck him, slowly, until I can feel his thighs quivering. He tastes good and strong after our ride. I guess I understand the primal appeal of getting naked with a hot, sweaty guy.

I look up at him through my lashes and he's

completely focused on me, his breathing labored, his eyes hooded as he stares down at me. I let his cock slide out of my mouth and he moans a little. "You can talk to me," I say, then go back to work.

"Holy hell, Drew," he says, thrusting into my mouth, but keeping his arms where I told him. "You look so hot right now with my cock in your mouth. You love it, don't you, sucking me off? You want me to come down your throat?"

I moan my approval at that particular idea.

He shudders. "You're going to get it, babe. You're going to get all of it, I promise. I'm not going to keep anything back."

I suck harder, loving how he's pumping into me, like he can't help it. Half a minute later, he stiffens and shouts as he lets himself go. I swallow most of it, spit the rest on the ground. I don't really know what got into me, except that being with Charlie makes me bold in ways I didn't know I could be.

I get off my knees, just then realizing how hard the ground I was kneeling on was. I stagger a little as I stand, but Charlie catches me, kisses me, gropes me through my sweats. "Jesus, you're so good," he says, and then he maneuvers to push me against the wall. I can feel the warm spot where his body heat seeped into the wood siding, and I sag against it. He sinks down. He's never blown me, but that's obviously what's happening now, and I experience a moment of panic. What if I don't smell good, taste good? What if he's put off by my size?

Okay, so far it's been more of a plus than a minus, but you never know.

But Charlie just sucks at the tip enthusiastically, then inches his way down my shaft. His mouth seems very wet —I can even hear the sloppy sound of my cock sliding through his spit, and the filthy noise gets me close, embarrassingly fast. I put my hand on the back of his head, forcing him a little farther, and he goes eagerly, mouth stretched around me. He looks blissed-out, his clothes completely rumpled, his hair a spiky mess. My cock in his mouth.

"Yeah, that's right, Charlie," I say. "Take me."

He gets another inch in, then gags, and the convulsion of his throat around my dick is scalding hot, but I don't want to hurt him. I try to pull back, but he grabs my hips and hauls me in again. He doesn't gag again, but he opens his mouth a little wider so I can hear the slip-slide of me fucking into him, and the faint choking noise he makes when I get close to the back of his throat.

It's all so dirty and good. He's being so good to me, giving me exactly what I want. What I need. And then I'm coming, suddenly, without warning, shooting right into the back of his throat. He gags again, and this time I do pull out, finishing in my hand, my cock sticky with his saliva and my come.

"Fuck." I collapse, so we're both on the ground. Charlie's breathing hard and I'm a little worried I hurt him, but he just looks at me with a goofy grin.

"You okay?" I ask, wiping my hand on my sweats and awkwardly pulling them up to cover myself.

"You're fucking big. But yeah, I'm fine. Are you—was that—" His grin fades. "Not the smoothest blow job ever."

It's weird seeing him insecure about something.

"It was amazing."

"Really? Because it looked and felt pretty fucking amazing. I just—I guess I need a little more practice taking you."

I swallow hard. Is that the sexiest sentence I've ever had directed at me?

Suddenly, Charlie's gaze shifts from my face to my legs. His lips curl back, and his entire demeanor changes. "Shit. Hold still," he orders, but not in an erotic way.

"What is it?" I look down at my legs, trying not to move. "A spider?" I'm not exactly afraid of them, but wouldn't want one crawling on me.

"A tick," he says grimly.

"Oh, gross." I can see it now, a tiny little black speck on my light gray sweats. I move to brush it off, but he stops me with a hand like a vise on my arm.

"Wait. We should collect it, just in case it bit you. That way, we can get it tested."

"It didn't bite me—it's on top of my clothes."

"You don't know that," he says tensely.

"I'm pretty sure. Can't we just squish it?" I'm not seeing what the big deal is, but then I remember and feel like a jerk. Brock died from some kind of Lyme disease complication, and you can get Lyme disease from tick bites. "I mean—um."

"Do you have a Ziploc bag in the house?"

"Yeah, in the cupboard under the microwave," I say.

He disappears. I stare at the little parasite, who's not moving, just resting ominously on my sweats, until he returns with a spoon and a little snack baggie.

Carefully, he scrapes the tick into the bag and seals it up.

"It can't have been there very long," I say. "Don't ticks have to be attached for a while to transmit any diseases?"

"Some tick-born illnesses can be transmitted within minutes, even though Lyme takes longer to transmit."

"Oh."

"It probably didn't bite you," he says, though he still sounds upset. "I'm just being extra cautious."

"Okay." I struggle with exactly what to say. "I guess you're pretty careful about ticks."

"I usually am," he says. "Yeah. I check after every walk, every ride. Even in the city, because there are some there. I should have reminded you."

"Well, we weren't exactly tromping around in the back woods," I say. "Just riding up and down my driveway."

"Doesn't matter," he says. "They're insidious little things. Sometimes you don't even know you've been bitten." His mouth is a sour pucker.

"Is that what happened to Brock? He didn't know?"

He nods slowly. "Yeah. We think he got infected with Lyme, didn't realize it, and suffered from a rare complication known as Lyme carditis that affected his heart. It's actually so rare that it's just a theory, and he died before he could get treatment. He'd had some general symptoms leading up to his death, but nothing that screamed Lyme disease. But when the doctors found out he'd been doing a lot of hiking on the Appalachian Trail that summer, they felt it was the most likely explanation."

"That's horrible."

"I mean, that's why we're doing the memorial ride, right? Not just to raise money, but to spread awareness. People mostly know to check for ticks and what to do if they notice they've been bitten by one, but there's still a lot of education that can be done. Not to mention the need for a vaccine, which has been in development for a while."

"Really? I didn't know that."

"Anyway, sorry for overreacting. I don't know what I'd do if—"

"Hey, I get it."

He gives me a grateful smile. We go inside, and he seals the bagged tick in a jar in the kitchen, presumably where we can access it should we need to.

Charlie goes back to the guest house to shower and change his clothes while I pull out ingredients for a stir-fry dinner that we planned to make together. His response to the tick situation makes perfect sense, yet it also scares me a little. I'm not the only one with issues in this relationship—and as good as things are, what if I can't be what he needs?

I've been worried about him leaving a Charlie-shaped hole in my life when he goes back to New York, but what if I'm the one who leaves a hole in his life? I know he's resilient, but I don't want to hurt him if I can help it. Unfortunately, I don't have my own life figured out enough to know if I can be a permanent part of his.

So far, I've been living moment to moment, enjoying this for what it is. It hasn't been that long, after all. And I mean, isn't this the dream? To be with a guy I can have hot sex with, then talk about work with, make dinner with, watch a movie with, fall asleep holding against my chest?

It's the kind of relationship I always wanted and the kind I told myself was unrealistic.

But Charlie is real. And if he's everything I ever wanted, does that mean the rug is going to be pulled out from under me soon, just like my dad would announce it was time for us to move whenever I was starting to settle into a new school and make real friends?

My dad's not here to call the shots anymore.

But I'm living in his house, surrounded by his things. Weighed down by our baggage.

Maybe I'm not as independent as I thought I was.

"MY ASS HURTS. Is my ass supposed to hurt this much?" Drew shifts his cute behind on the seat of his bike as we cruise around the residential neighborhood near downtown Rosedale.

"You'll get used to it," I say, "and if you want, we can get you a wider, softer seat. But honestly, you're doing great." I'm not surprised he's a little sore. After our session yesterday, today we rode all the way from his house to town, practicing our road etiquette. It's a lot if you aren't used to a hard seat.

"Is this why your ass is so perky?" He shifts again and groans. "Because you've hardened it into one big callus?"

"I'm not sure if that's a compliment or not." I laugh and pull to a stop next to a sidewalk. Drew comes up next to me, color in his cheeks. He's wearing an *X-Files* T-shirt and a pair of joggers, making me feel slightly silly in my tight racing-style shirt and shorts, but that's what I have.

He eyes my ass and gives me a sly grin. "I'm not complaining," he says.

"Good to know. What about a break? I'll buy you lunch."

"Yes, please. I'm going to need sustenance if we have to ride all the way home."

"It's two miles. You've got this."

We navigate to Main Street and use my lock to string our bikes and helmets up together at a bike rack in front of a secondhand store. "Don't forget to hydrate," I remind Drew, who takes a swig of water from his bottle. "What do you feel like?"

"Like I'm going to be even more sore tomorrow," he jokes.

"I'll give you a massage later."

"It's a deal." He smiles at me, and I sway toward him, but stop. I don't know how he feels about PDA, and I know I tend to lose my head a little when we touch. Better to keep my hands to myself.

"What about the coffee shop?" I suggest, turning away from him. "They have food, too."

"Sure," he says easily. "But I'm buying."

"What? Why?"

"Call it payment for the private bike lessons. You're a really good teacher, Charlie," he says, and I detect nothing but sincerity in his voice.

"Oh. Thanks." I wonder if lessons are something someone who owned a bike shop would offer, then catch myself. The bike event is what I should be thinking about right now, not some far-fetched entrepreneurial fantasy.

We walk the short block down to Hot Brew, the caffeine purveyor of choice around these parts, according to Jack.

"Small town alert," I say when we walk into the clean black-and-white tiled space. Jack is sitting at a table by the window, his laptop open in front of him, a large white mug and a crumb-filled plate at his elbow. Since he doesn't look up from his computer, I walk over and wave my hand in front of his face.

"Oh, hey, Charlie," he says. "Sorry, I'm working."

"Sorry for bothering you, then."

"Nah, it's okay. I could use a break. Hey, Drew." Jack gets up and stretches. "What are you two up to?"

"We rode here all the way from my house," Drew says with pride. "And I hadn't ridden a bike in years before yesterday."

"Did you now? That's very cool," he says. "Getting some lunch?"

"Yeah. What do you like here?"

"Everything," he says unhelpfully. "But the salads are really good. Or the grilled cheese."

Drew makes a happy noise. "Grilled cheese sounds amazing right now."

"Can we get you anything?" I ask Jack, but he shakes his head.

"No, I was just trying to get through a little story problem, but I think I figured it out. Pete was getting sick of me, so I thought I'd give him some space."

"I find that very hard to believe," I say. He and Pete are the most in sync couple since...since me and Brock. The thought no longer fills me with a pang. I glance at Drew. He's not a replacement for Brock. No one could be. But he's definitely good for me. And he's definitely not a consolation prize.

"It's all good," Jack says. "But maybe I'll get him a pastry for later."

We all get in line behind a young couple standing close enough to seem fused at the hip. The goth woman waiting on them looks familiar.

"Do I know her?" I whisper to Jack.

"That's Meadow. Her girlfriend Melissa works at the bookshop," he says, adding that she was at his wedding.

"Oh, right." I remember meeting Meadow at the wedding, but not Melissa. Must be the same woman I ran into on the street a couple of days ago.

"Jack, who have you brought me today?" Meadow asks as the couple in front of us takes their croissants to a table and we advance to the counter.

"You remember Charlie from my wedding? He's the one organizing the memorial bike race."

"And the one who came to Melissa's rescue on Friday." She smiles at me. "Thanks for that, by the way."

"Anytime. Did you take a look at her chain?"

"Oh yeah, I got her chain tightened up real nice." She gives me a wink and I laugh.

"Am I missing something?" Jack says.

Drew chuckles. "Bike people all have dirty minds, I think."

"That explains it. Well, Drew, meet Meadow. She keeps Hot Brew functioning."

Drew's forehead crinkles. "Actually, I think we've met. You were at my dad's funeral. David Hersh?"

Meadow's face loses its playfulness, but not her smile. "I remember meeting you, Drew. David talked about you all the time. You work in movies or TV, he said?"

"Movies," he says. "Dad must have been a regular."

"He came in most Saturdays, after he hit the tag sales. He always brought me any Patricia Highsmith novels he found because he knew she was my favorite. Nice man," she says kindly. "I didn't know you were back in Rosedale."

"I've actually been here for a while," Drew says hesitantly. "But I've never been in here before."

Meadow's penciled-on eyebrows fly north. "You've never been to Hot Brew?"

"An oversight I am happy to rectify," he says solemnly.

"Well, good," she says, seemingly appeased. "What can I get you?"

Jack advises us on the menu, and we end up with two grilled cheese sandwiches and a beet salad to share.

"What's pumpkin spice hot chocolate?" Drew asks.

"An abomination against nature," Meadow says dryly. "But the customers seem to like it. We only carry it through the end of October, then it's peppermint hot chocolate." She does a full-body shudder.

"Too rich for my blood. Black coffee for me," I say.

Drew bites his lip in a way I find utterly endearing. "Will you break up with me if I order a pumpkin spice hot chocolate?"

Jack snorts and Meadow sighs, but I'm so flabbergasted by Drew's choice of words that it takes me a moment to formulate a response, during which time Drew fidgets with the hem of his shirt.

He thinks whatever we are is serious enough that if it ended, it would be breaking up.

Awesome.

"Babe, it would take a lot more than horrible taste in seasonal beverages to get me to break up with you."

Immediately, he says, "Hey!" But then he smiles softly. I hope he liked my answer. I sway toward him again, but Meadow interrupts us.

"Okay, one black coffee, one pumpkin spice hot chocolate. For here, right, guys?"

Drew pays, just like he said he would, and stuffs a large handful of bills into the tip jar. Jack closes his computer, puts it in a messenger bag. "I gotta get home. Nice running into you two."

He hugs us goodbye, then Drew watches him leave, a grin on his face.

"What's got you so smiley?" I ask, smiling to myself as we take the table Jack just vacated. Must be catching.

"Oh, it's just neat to run into people I know here in town. It makes me feel like, I don't know, I'm actually part of the community here."

"That's great, Drew." I want to ask him if he's okay after the reminder of his dad's funeral, but my phone is buzzing in my pocket. When I pull it out, I see it's Paloma calling me. She must be back from her conference.

Before I accept the call, I get an idea. "Want to blow Paloma's mind?"

"Sure, I guess," Drew says, cocking his head questioningly.

I punch the button to turn the audio call into a video one and wait for the connection.

Then the screen of my phone shows my oldest friend's face: light brown skin, straight black hair, pointy chin, fashionable cat-eye glasses.

"Hi gorgeous," I say.

"Spill. Now," she says, her voice clear over the speaker. I'd feel bad about using my speaker in a public place, but we're the only ones on this side of the coffee shop. "How did you find Andy? What's he like? I can't believe you haven't sent me any pictures."

"Andy is Drew now, and you can see for yourself." I scoot my chair as close to Drew as I can, then move the phone so he's in the frame with me. Drew gives her a shy wave, and her screech has me hitting the volume down button as fast as I can.

I glance around Hot Brew, but no one's paying us any attention.

"Hi, Paloma," Drew says. "How've you been?"

"I'm doing fantastic, thank you, *Drew*." She puts an emphasis on his name. "I like that, by the way. Drew suits you. You look great. And Charlie just randomly rented your guest house? You live in Connecticut now? I'm serious. I want details."

"Well, Charlie's sister is my assistant editor. We're working on a movie together." Drew gives her the abbreviated version of Allie arranging for me to stay in his guest house, leaving out the matchmaking part, and he stops before he tells her that we've already escaped the friend zone.

"So you're a video editor? That is completely cool.

Where are you guys right now? The background is kind of fuzzy."

"We're in Hot Brew, Rosedale's coffee shop."

"Oh, I think I've been there. Seb and I went to the Rosedale Art Center for an art show a couple of years ago. Cute town."

"And you and Seb live in Atlanta and got married? That's unbelievable," Drew says.

"Atlanta is still growing on us, but we both got jobs here we couldn't turn down. And yes, Seb grew on me, too." She grins. "He's on a run, but I'm sure he says hi."

"When are you coming up north?" I ask. It's been too long since I've seen them.

"I'm not sure. But I miss you. And Andy—I mean, Drew. Sorry."

"It's okay." Drew shrugs.

"I know I'm on video phone and there's zero privacy, so you can ignore this if you want—but you, like, know that you both had a crush on each other in high school, right?"

"Paloma." I groan.

"What? I'm just saying, I did my best to push you guys together but then A—Drew, left town, and I lost my chance to be matchmaker."

"As a matter of fact, that information came to light without you. Apparently, Charlie Linden wanted to kiss me," Drew says, as if the concept is completely outlandish.

"And Andy Hersh wanted to kiss me," I say, a bit smugly, because yeah. I give in to my next impulse, because I just can't not drop this final bomb on her, and lean over and kiss Drew quickly on the lips.

I'm glad I lowered the volume earlier because the noise Paloma emits is almost as shrill as a gym teacher's whistle. "Oh my god, oh my god," she says, covering her face with her hands. "You two are—what?"

"Kissing, obviously," I say.

"I knew it! I knew you two would be good together." She sounds as jubilant as if she'd just won a Nobel Peace Prize.

"You were right," Drew says. His cheeks are a little pink, but he looks happy. We exchange a glance. "We are good together."

"Very good," I agree.

TWENTY-THREE
DREW

A FEW DAYS after our bike ride into town, I finally complete the rough cut of the film. The export will take hours, then I'll upload it so the director, Phoebe, can watch it and pass judgment. Next week, she and I will meet to discuss the changes that need to be made in order to achieve the final cut.

With the edit out of my hands for now, I have time to attend to some of the piles on my desk that keep growing. I put on a podcast, sort through a stack of mail, and burn out after opening two bills and a cold letter from a local Realtor who would love to help me get top dollar for my property. I'm not ready to think about that and I push away from my desk with a guilty sigh.

In procrastination mode, I make a snack, cuddle Cinnamon until he wriggles out of my arms, and wander into the library. I should really go through the books. Someone mentioned that the Rosedale Library takes donations for their book sale. I have a feeling that's where my dad probably picked up most of these books, but no matter.

I glance at one shelf and am able to cull half the books right away. That feels good, but now I need a box. I go to the front room, with its stacks of boxes I've yet to even touch. With trepidation, I open the flaps of the first one, hoping I won't find anything furry—dead or alive—inside. But it just seems to be a box of paperwork from my dad's job, dated from at least ten years back. I should take them to be shredded, or maybe just burn them in the fire pit I was thinking it would be nice to get for the back porch to huddle around as the nights get colder.

The next box has more kitchen stuff in it. How many slotted spoons does one person need, honestly? I'm more interested in the couple of mugs inside—I'm always leaving mugs around the house and never have any in the kitchen when I want to make tea. One is plain white, but the next stops me cold. It's a Hot Brew mug, white with their logo on it in black and the tagline Some Like it Hot underneath in red. It's a cute mug.

For some reason, I'm crying.

My dad lived in Rosedale for over a decade. According to Meadow, he went to Hot Brew countless times. I never got to go there with him.

I was too stubborn to visit him here—too hurt by his inability to see how much he'd hurt me by finally choosing the one thing I actually got down on my non-religious knees and prayed for as a kid.

And now he's gone and I'm never going to get that chance again.

I'm angry at him, and I'm angry at myself. What am I doing? Why am I even still here in this house that's full of memories I never got to share with him? It doesn't make sense—I should be in Los Angeles, in my comfortable little apartment with my comfortable little life. A few friends, my work. Watching movies by myself, eating delivery alone. I knew how to do that life.

I don't know how to do this, to be here.

The front doorbell rings and I know it can only be Charlie. I pat away the hot tears from my cheeks, wipe my nose on the hem of my T-shirt, then open the door.

"Oh, babe, what's wrong?" Charlie says the second he sees my face.

"Nothing," I say, which is so ridiculous that I laugh, but my laugh is full of mucus from crying, and I cough and then hide the disgusting mess of my face in my hands.

"Babe, what is it?" Charlie comes in and shuts the door, ushers me to the offensively salmon downstairs bathroom. He tears off a handful of toilet paper and hands it to me so I can scrub my face and blow my nose. He waits patiently for me to meet his gaze. "Tell me about it." His face is pinched with worry, and I hate making him upset because this has nothing to do with him. It's all about me and my messed-up feelings.

"I was going through a couple of my dad's boxes," I start.

Charlie lights up at that, as if proud of me.

"I didn't get very far," I caution him, "and I found—this is so stupid—I found a mug from Hot Brew, and it just made me realize that I'll never get to go there with him and I should have visited him here and I shouldn't have been such a stubborn son of a bitch and he's gone and he'll never get to know..."

I stop, shocked by what I was about to say.

"Never get to know what?" Charlie asks encouragingly.

"I never got to tell him that it was okay. That despite always being the new kid, the nerdy lowest of the social strata at every new school, I turned out all right. He never —I think he always felt like he'd messed me up. It kept him from reaching out. From getting close. And I let him stay at a distance."

As I talk, I realize it's true. I may be a long way from getting over some of this stuff, but I did turn out okay, and I hope my dad knew that.

"I spent a lot of years just plain mad. But now...I really miss him. And I'd take a relationship with him over the perfect childhood."

"I wish you could have that," Charlie says softly. He doesn't say that my dad knew I loved him, or that none of this matters now that he's gone. He just stands with me in this hideous bathroom and lets me talk.

"Anyway, I know I've been obtuse about some of this. It probably seems obvious to you—that I should have seen it coming."

"Hey, we all respond to grief in different ways," he says lightly. "It's really okay, Drew."

Grief. Such a simple word, but it holds so many meanings, so many emotions, so many different experiences.

For the first time, something else occurs to me. "Do you think one of the reasons my dad moved so much was because of his grief about my mom? We didn't start moving until after she died—I always got the feeling he was looking for something he could never find."

"Maybe he was looking for the kind of home he'd had with her?" Charlie guesses. "Or maybe he was running away from his grief. I don't know."

"I don't know, either." But thinking about my dad's choices after my mom died makes me wish I could tell him to his face that even though it was hard, I forgive him. "I wonder if he found what he was looking for here?" I look around the small room. "The ugliest bathroom in America."

Charlie snorts out a laugh, and the mood is broken. But he doesn't let me off the hook that easily. "Either he found what he was looking for or he decided to stop running away. Either way, he made a choice to stay here."

"And you think I should make the same choice?" I ask.

"I think you should make *a* choice," he says carefully.

I think I want to choose Rosedale, this house, this life. Charlie.

But how do I know if that's the right thing?

A few weeks ago, I didn't even know Charlie. I was content in my isolation bubble, no one to worry about, no one to worry about me. Suddenly it's all too much, too fast.

I push past him into the hallway. I need air. I need to get out. I make for the front door.

"Drew?" Charlie calls.

I go out the door, leave it open. I take deep gulps of cool October air. I'm chilly in my thin shirt. My driveway is a river of leaves—the trees are starting to lose them in droves. The next big storm that comes through will take down a ton, leaving some of the branches bare.

Winter will be here before we know it.

"Hey, babe." Charlie's at my side, his voice soft, concerned. He reaches out, puts an arm around me, encourages me to put my head on his shoulder.

I snake my arms around his waist. He feels so good—so warm and alive. It's not too late to tell him how I feel about him.

But it would help if I knew what I was feeling. Is this lust? Is this love?

Is it just a teenage crush we're taking to the nth degree?

I nuzzle into his neck, tightening my hold on his middle. He must have just come in from a ride because he's wearing his biking clothes and the small of his back is still a bit damp from the exertion. I can smell his piney deodorant, which I like, and his sweat, which I like even better.

I don't know what I'm doing—that much is clear—but I know what I want right now. I want Charlie. I want his hands and his mouth and his body. I want him to make me feel good and I want to make him come so hard he won't be able to remember anything except my name.

I want to live in this moment forever, where we're touching each other and that's all that matters.

"Come to bed with me?" I ask, whispering the words

into Charlie's collarbone, then kissing him there in the hopes of sealing the deal.

"All right," he says. "Yes."

And I lead him upstairs without letting him go.

DREW IS CLEARLY WORKING through some tough things, and part of me knows I should be reminding him that it'll take time, that he should probably talk to a professional, that it's not always a good idea to stop yourself from experiencing your negative emotions. But if he wants comfort, if he wants sex—it's also not the worst idea in the world.

We hold hands walking through the house, up the stairs, and into his room. His bed looks like it hasn't been touched since we rolled out of it together this morning. At this point, I'm basically using the guest house as a closet and a place to store my bicycle. I didn't mean to move in with my landlord, it just kind of happened.

Just like this entire relationship just kind of happened.

Drew fell into my life. Or did I fall into his? Either way, I wasn't looking for someone to share a bed with, let alone someone new to share my life with. But I feel like

I've found someone who fits both descriptions, and I can only be grateful.

I take off my shirt and shorts, pull Drew onto the bed on top of me, and kiss him slowly, imbuing the kiss with all of my gratitude for simply finding him. In this wild world where most people don't even get to have one epic love, I feel like I've been given the chance to have two.

Because as Drew covers me with his body, kissing his way down the column of my throat and over my chest, I'm pretty sure the tender, almost painful ache in my heart is love.

I know what being in love feels like. This is almost the same, but different, because it's Drew. He's different. He's someone I want to know forever.

And he's lapping his tongue over the crown of my semi-hard cock. I hiss and arch into him, but his mouth on me isn't what I want today. I gently reverse our positions so he's lying on the mattress. Slowly, I undress him, not put off by his puffy red eyes. He loved his dad. He's hurting. I get it. He's just as beautiful to me this way—his bleeding heart on display—as he is any other day.

When he's naked, I kiss my way from his ankle to his hip. His cock rests in the crease of his thigh. Neither of us is all the way hard. I'm content to take things slow, to show him that it doesn't have to be hot and heavy between us all the time.

Going slow is a risky act—one that declares to the universe that we're deliberately taking all the time we want. We may not be able to choose how much time we're each allotted, but we have right now, and I'm determined to spend every second I can with the beautiful, kind, funny man in my arms.

With that in mind, I start stroking his skin. It's not quite a massage—I just want to feel him, the curve of his muscles, the knobs of his joints, the soft wisps of hair on his forearms, his shins. I sweep my hands up his thighs; he widens his legs slightly, and I trace the sensitive valleys of his pelvis, the lightly furred sac that sits heavy between his legs. I roll his balls in my hand, and his cock twitches. It's no longer lying to the side, but is fully erect, pointing up his body, the tip of it grazing the dark line of hair leading from his navel to his bush. He's just the right amount of hairy for me. He doesn't trim, so there's plenty of soft, dark hair for me to stroke and worship. I get down between his legs, eager to continue my exploration, forcing myself to stay steady and slow.

It's time for my nose and tongue to get in on the action. I press my face under his balls, that dark, secret place that I'm allowed to be, and breathe. He's warm down there, and he smells deliciously musky.

"Charlie," he says on a gasp when I lift his balls out of the way and lick the sensitive patch of skin right behind. He swivels his hips. "I should have showered."

"You're perfect," I reassure him, tasting him there again. I don't go all the way to his rim—maybe another day—instead I lick my way upward again, over his sac, over the base of his cock, up the shaft, to the tip, swiping the salty pre-come off his slit with a satisfied little moan.

"You're incredible," he says.

"Thank you." I can't help being a little smug. Usually, I end up a total wreck in our lovemaking sessions due to the intense way Drew has taken me apart, but today it's my turn to have my way with him.

Because we're taking our time, I leave him long enough to get the lube from the drawer and come back to find him looking at me curiously.

"No blow job?" he says, sounding disappointed.

"I had something else in mind."

He raises his eyebrows. "Like what?"

We've talked about anal, and it turns out it isn't Drew's favorite sex act. I enjoy ass play, and Drew's had his fingers in me more than once since we started having sex—the man is a wizard at finding my prostate—but as for an entire cock, well, Drew's is a little intimidating. I'm open to it in the future—again, I've got to trust that we'll have time to get there. Drew told me he's not a huge fan of bottoming, which is fine, though I wonder if maybe he just hasn't had a partner who's been able to make it good for him. I know that's totally egotistical, but it could be true. None of what Drew's mentioned about his exes have made them sound like particularly good lovers. But I could be biased.

Or maybe not.

Either way, I want to try to make Drew feel as good as he makes me in this area. Not because I'm desperate to top him—literally everything else we've done together has been so good I've hardly been wishing for something else —but because he deserves to feel amazing.

"Let me touch you here?" I ask as I press one lubed finger to the pucker of his hole. "I'll go slow, and you can stop me any time."

"Okay," he says. He doesn't sound like he's

consenting because he thinks that's what I want to hear. To the contrary, he's breathless with arousal. I circle the spot, getting it nice and wet. It's just another part of his body I want to feel, to memorize. He widens his legs even more, slides his feet back, and bends his knees, baring himself to me entirely.

"Holy hell, you're so hot," I say, glad it's daytime and I have the afternoon light to see by. Drew's hands are bunched into fists in the sheets. I keep circling his rim, adding more lube, feeling the delicate skin quiver against my finger, almost as if it's opening up to me. "Does that feel good?"

"Yeah," he says immediately. "You're good at this. Some guys just rush—ah—through it." He gasps as I stop and press my finger against his opening.

"Can I go inside?" I ask, keeping my movements deliberate and firm, and adding even more lube in the process.

"Y-yeah," he says, blowing out a noisy breath as I breach him practically in slow motion. I push inside to the first knuckle and stop, letting him get used to the feeling of something inside him.

"Okay?"

He nods. "Okay." But his entire body is tight as a bungee cord stretched to its limit, and I ease my finger out, then lean up the bed so I can kiss him, wet and deep. We keep kissing until I feel him relax beneath me.

"Better," I say. "I just want to make you feel good."

"It's good," he says. He smiles at me, his eyes a little hazy. "It's intense."

"Yeah. How do you think it was the other day when you were milking my prostate? I felt high."

"That was hot," he says, as if he's remembering how much I shot that night. I came so hard and for so long the sheets were drenched and we had to put on a fresh set.

"Fucking hot. Now let me do my thing," I say.

He makes a visible attempt to relax, and I go back to his hole, circling, putting pressure on his perineum until I can practically see his cock weeping pre-come. Then I finally put my finger back inside him. He shouts when I add a second finger. He takes me easily, so I know I'm not hurting him, but he must be feeling the stretch because he wriggles his hips, the side effect of which is him forcing my fingers in a little deeper.

He swears and I stop, letting him adjust.

"Wanna touch yourself?" I ask. I have the bottle of lube in my free hand, and I wave it over his straining cock.

"Um. If I touch myself, I'm gonna come." He's back to clutching the sheets in his fists again. "Is that how you want me to come?"

I shudder, suddenly aware of how rock hard I am, and how open he's being with me. We always take turns setting the pace, but in the end I usually let him take us to the finish line, since he's pretty fucking spectacular at it. But right now, I want something else. "No, wait."

Instead of lubing up his cock, I lube up my own, drizzling too much on my erection, but not caring. I toss the bottle to the side, push his knees down, and take my fingers out of his ass. "Put your legs together."

He does, and I position myself over him, sliding my

wet cock in between his upper thighs, just under his balls.

"Can you keep it tight for me?" I ask, meeting his eyes with mine. His pupils are blown out, and now his cheeks are redder from our sex than his crying jag.

He nods, his lips parted. I kiss him, and he squeezes his thighs together, making a tight, hot channel for me to rock into. It's a good kind of pressure, and just slippery enough to make the slide easy, but not so sloppy I can't keep up a rhythm. It feels incredible pumping into him, but not into him, the friction causing my orgasm to build frustratingly quickly. I slow my hips, keep my thrusts shallow and steady.

"That feels good?" he asks.

"So good," I grit out. "So fucking good, you have no idea."

"You want to try—I mean, you want to get inside me?" he asks hesitantly.

"Oh, babe." I want that, but not if it's not what he really wants. "This is good," I assure him, building the rhythm up again.

"Okay, just—um. Can you put on a condom?"

I immediately stop, pull myself free of his thighs. "Oh god, yes, I'm sorry," I say. I'm negative—I even showed him the results of my last physical—and he told me he's negative, too, though he joked he'd have to be a much more organized person to be able to prove it to me. We haven't used condoms for oral, but it doesn't matter why he wants me to wear one right now—if he wants me to, I'm doing it.

"It's okay, Charlie," he says. "I just—"

"No, it's fine." I know there's a condom in the drawer, so I put it on, then add more lube. Despite the interruption, my cock is hard as ever. Drew turns me on so much, it would take more than a request to wear a condom to make me lose my erection.

"Okay, yeah." He stays in position, legs together, his own cock looking angry red. "Lube, please."

I initially think he means more lube on the condom, but he moves the bottle in my hand toward his cock. "Please."

I squirt a dollop on him, and he sighs as he spreads it over himself. But then he takes his hand away and guides my cock back to his crotch.

"Keep going," he grunts, and I don't have to be told twice.

I rock into that slick, hot space again, the sensation a little bit less intense but more slippery with the condom on. He doesn't touch himself, but his face is screwed up tight, like it's taking all his self-control to keep his hands off himself, and his red flush has spread down his chest.

"Are you close?" he asks.

"Yeah, babe, so close. You feel so good."

"Okay." He widens his legs a fraction then, so I lose the tunnel of flesh I was thrusting into, but before I can figure out how to pivot from here, he grabs my cock, lifts his hips, and guides the blunt head of it against his hole.

"Is this okay?" he asks me. "Can you just go a little bit inside? Just the tip?"

"Yeah." I nudge his opening, still wet from the lube I fingered into it before. "Yeah, just the tip." I get it inside, and he gasps, and then his hand is flying, stroking his cock frantically, while the hot, tight grip on the head of my cock sets off my orgasm, fierce and sharp. I run the razor edge of thrusting forward as my cock pulses come out into the condom, but not pushing too far inside his channel. It's different, and potent. And my own orgasm seems secondary when Drew's begins, causing him to simultaneously clamp down hard on my cock and shoot ribbons of creamy come all over his belly, some streaking all the way up to his nipples.

"Holy hell," I gasp.

He's twitching as the last spurts of come seep through his fingers and around his cock. I grab the base of the condom and pull out as carefully as I can.

"How was that?" he asks.

"That's what I should be asking you. Fuck, Drew. You wanted that?"

"I wanted it. And it felt...extraordinary." He smiles at me, as if he's learned something new about himself.

I smile back. I wanted to make him feel as good as I possibly could, and I mentally give myself a gold star.

Comfort sex for the win.

I perfunctorily clean us up, kiss him on the mouth. "That was so good," I say. "I—"

I almost want to tell him I love him. But it's already been an emotional day. And besides, we have time.

"YOU ARE AN ABSOLUTE GENIUS, Drew, honestly. We couldn't have loved the cut more," Phoebe, the director of the horror movie I've been working on for the last two months, gushes at me from her sunny office in Santa Monica, California, while I huddle in my heaviest sweater. The heat didn't kick on this morning, and I have a call out to Lucas, since he doubles as my HVAC guy, but in the meantime Charlie's working in the guest house, which is on a different system, and I'm shivering in my office. It's the first truly cold morning we've had this fall—in the forties outside, and though it's supposed to warm up to the sixties by the afternoon, I'm feeling the chill.

"Thanks, Phoebe," I say. "That's good to hear."

"I especially love the way you cut the conversation in the diner with the quick cuts. It's not exactly what we talked about, but I adore it."

"I based that on a suggestion from my assistant editor, actually," I say, remembering it was Alyson's idea to speed up the pace in the emotionally charged scene. "Alyson Cross."

"Give her props from me," Phoebe says. "Now, of course, we have to make some changes. And I have some temp music I need you to drop in so I can share it with the composer."

"No problem." I knew there would be changes, no matter how much she loved the cut. It's all part of the process. "I'll look for your notes and the music cues."

"Yeah, I'll get them to you by the end of the day. Oh, I almost forgot to tell you, it's looking good for South by Southwest."

"That's great news. Keep me posted."

"Will do. Thanks again, Drew. By the way, if you're coming to L.A. anytime soon, let me know and we'll get together."

We end the call, and I shoot a quick message off to Alyson, letting her know we did good. Lucas texts me that he won't make it until closer to five. Phoebe's words of praise echo in my head as I help myself to the dregs of the coffee in the pot. Screw it, she loved the cut. I'm treating myself to lunch and one of those pumpkin spice hot chocolates at Hot Brew. I switch out my slippers for my sneakers, grab my keys, and walk over to the guest house.

It's almost warmer outside than in, and it's definitely warmer inside the little guest house, where Charlie's at the kitchen table in front of his laptop. He's got earbuds in and holds up a finger when I get inside. "Sounds good. No—I'm supposed to be off this week. I'll be back in the office Tuesday. If it can't wait, ask Rahul if he can take it on. Okay. Thanks, Joe."

He clicks a button on his computer and takes out his earbuds. "Work call, even though I'm on PTO." He sighs. "I'm so over my job."

"And yet you'll be back in the office on Tuesday," I say. It's a statement of fact, but I wince as it comes out of my mouth, slightly bitter.

The bike event is this weekend. Charlie's supposed to go home on Monday.

He hasn't said anything about what he's going to do after that. Until now. And we definitely haven't talked about what we're going to do—long distance? Go back to being friends?

"I, uh, I'm going to Hot Brew," I say. "You want anything?" I was going to ask him if he wanted to come with me, but suddenly I'm shy. Maybe this really is just a temporary thing that's going to end in a few days. Maybe that's what Charlie thought it was all along, and I'm just the oblivious bastard who was too busy living in the moment to realize it wasn't supposed to last.

"You going to ride your bike there?" Charlie asks with a smile.

"No, I'm going to drive," I say stiffly. "My car. Like a regular person." It's kind of mean, but my emotions are all over the place. Phoebe loved the cut, but there's a ton more work to do on it. She mentioned the next time I'm in L.A. Well, maybe I should head back out there. Most of my stuff's still in my apartment, the apartment I continue to pay rent on while I knock around in this falling-down farmhouse. Charlie's going back to the city. Neither of us really belong here in Rosedale, no matter how much it truly started to feel like home these last few weeks.

"What's wrong?" he says, pushing back from the table and taking a few steps toward me. I back up involuntarily and he frowns.

"Nothing."

"Didn't you have your meeting with the director this morning? What happened? Did they like it?"

"Yeah, actually, Phoebe loved it. She has notes, of course, but overall we did good. Alyson and me, I mean. She's been a rock star."

He smiles. "Not surprised to hear it. She's awesome."

"On that, we're agreed," I say.

He scrunches up his forehead. "Does that mean on other things we aren't agreed? Seriously, babe, what's going on?"

"Don't—don't call me that."

His face falls and I get a chill despite the heater working fine in here and my thick sweater.

"It's just—I think I need to go back to L.A." There, that way he doesn't have to feel bad about going back to New York and resuming his life where he left off.

"For work?" he asks.

"Yeah. Sort of. I should check on my apartment. See some of my friends."

"Wait—you still have an apartment there?"

"Uh, yeah." I either need to renew the lease for another year or vacate in thirty days. Maybe this is the push I needed to finally make a decision.

"Seriously? So you're just—you're leaving?"

It sounds so final when he says it.

"I—I don't know. Being here was only supposed to be while I went through my dad's things and got the house ready to sell. I should have already put it on the market." All that is true, even if it leaves me feeling hollow.

"But you love it here," he says. "Or are you going to be, like, bicoastal or something?"

I can't stand this feeling, as though everything I've put off thinking about is coming back to bite me. I don't want to leave Rosedale, to leave Charlie. But if he's gone, and Dad's gone, and all of this was just some waking dream, me thinking I could have the rom-com ending, then I have to face it.

I had a life in Los Angeles. A small life. But a safe one. This beautiful fall, being with Charlie, just delayed the inevitable. Rosedale isn't for me. This house is too big, too much work. Since Charlie rode up to my front door on his bicycle, I've been living for the moment.

Well, this moment fucking sucks.

"I'm not going to be bicoastal. I'm going to sell the house."

"But this is your home now," Charlie says, sounding unsure.

I think about rattling around in the farmhouse when Charlie's back in the city, just me and Cinnamon, and I shudder. It sounds unbearably lonely.

"I just don't know if I'm cut out for this."

"B—" Charlie stops before he can say it, flares his nostrils. "Drew. I don't understand where this is coming from. Wake up. Rosedale is your home now. Your dad is gone. He can never make up for all the scars of your childhood, but he left you something amazing—he left you this beautiful home, one that suits you down to the ground. And if you don't want it, well—that's your choice. But don't lose it because you're scared to take it."

"I'm not scared," I retort, even though maybe that's exactly what I am. I'm scared that without Charlie, I'm just a sad, lonely man with a cat. At least in L.A. I have friends. If I put my shingle out, I'd have more work than I could handle.

"Then why are you running away?"

"Look, this is really none of your business," I say. "These last few weeks have been great, but we're not really—"

"What?"

"We're just two people who knew each other for three months in high school. We fell into this—two guys with a mutual attraction. But our lives are going in different directions, and that's okay." Charlie shouldn't have to apologize for choosing his normal life over me.

"Are you saying this was just sex?" he asks.

"No, but it's not like we're going to base life decisions on hooking up for a few weeks. Right?" I can't expect him to leave his life in New York and start over with me here. That would be ridiculous.

He's silent for a long minute, during which I have plenty of time to berate myself for all my wasted hopes and dreams. And then the final nail in the coffin. "I guess not."

"Right." That makes sense. "So, anyway. Um." I guess this is it. The ignominious ending to the best relationship I ever had. "Bye."

"You aren't leaving today, are you?" he asks, sounding incredulous. "Saturday is the big day. I thought you were going to be there."

I had been looking forward to cheering Charlie on, to taking photos and videos to document the day, to making sure he got the flowers he deserved for pulling off such a huge event. But what's the point if he's just leaving? "Maybe it's better if I'm not."

"Oh." His face looks pinched, as if maybe he's trying not to cry.

"I'm going to go now," I say, and he flinches. "I mean, not go to L.A. Just to Hot Brew. I guess."

"Okay." He's looking at the floor, and I back out the door and walk to my house, feeling numb. I hadn't gone over there to break up with him, yet somehow that's what I've done.

But he hadn't stopped me.

I get in the car and drive downtown on autopilot. I can't face my house, or texts from Alyson. I can't even face Meadow at Hot Brew, or risk running into Jack or Pete or Beck. I keep driving, straight out of Rosedale and onto the country road that leads to Midville, the next town over. It's bigger, with more stores, even a movie theater. I pass it, then pull a U-turn and park in the big lot next to the four-screen theater.

Movies have always been my refuge, comforting me when I'm sad, or worried, or depressed. They're dependable—my favorites always stay the same, the same lines in the same order. No matter what chaos was going on in my life growing up, I could count on my favorite movies to deliver the same experience over and over again.

And new movies get me out of my head, offering a respite from real life via a hundred minutes of escape.

And boy, do I need an escape.

I go inside, buy a ticket for the next movie that's playing. It's a monster movie. Perfect. I get popcorn, ignoring the stab to my chest when I spot gummy bears in the candy rack. So what if Charlie was the best thing to ever happen to me? So what if I ended things before they could get messy?

I sit in the dark theater, viciously pleased that I'm the only one there at one p.m. on a Thursday. Being alone in the dark is what I deserve.

Alone in the dark is what I am.

TWENTY-SIX

CHARLIE

I LOOK out my door a few minutes after Drew's departure. It took me that long to get over the shock of what just happened and make my feet move.

His car is gone.

He did it. He really left.

Okay, so maybe he didn't walk out of my life like my dad did. He didn't drop dead, like Brock.

But he's gone, and it feels like he's never coming back.

Even if he does, it'll never be the same.

And I don't know what I did wrong.

But I can't think about it. Even though I consider getting on my bike and racing over to Hot Brew to demand he give me—us—another chance, I have too many last-minute details to take care of for the event on Saturday. The volunteer training is tomorrow, so I have to sort out the rider and volunteer T-shirts and the signage. Everything is being staged at Jack and Pete's garage, bless them. The Brock Harris Memorial Ride for Lyme Disease Awareness and Prevention is the most important thing right now. I don't have time to worry about my love life.

"SO THAT'S ALL the signs for the route. When are we going to put them up?" Pete asks, labeling the cardboard box of route arrows and markers.

"Tomorrow afternoon. I have four people assigned to that," I say, looking at my volunteer spreadsheet. "Thanks again for helping me with this."

"No problem. Jack said he can help more tomorrow, too," Pete says. "I think I'm going to make a cup of tea. You want one?"

"Sure." We've gone through most of the items on my to-do list—the rest will have to wait until tomorrow. Saturday, the day of the event, will be the longest day— I'll have to be up early to make sure the road closures go into effect when they're supposed to, and then welcome everyone. Public speaking isn't my favorite thing, but it'll be worth it to see so many people gathered together in one place to honor Brock. His parents are coming in from Florida for the event, as are some of our friends from the city. Jack and Pete, obviously. I saw Melissa's name on the list of people signed up for the road race portion. The ten-mile ride is an open ride, so I don't know exactly how many people will be participating in that, but we have over a hundred riders signed up with pledges, so that's exciting.

I should be over the moon about the event finally happening.

Instead, as I follow Pete from the garage into his and Jack's lovely lived-in kitchen, I feel drained.

"Will you tell me what's wrong now?" Pete asks as he puts water into an electric kettle. "Black, green, or chamomile?"

"Green. And what makes you think something's wrong?"

"Well, you normally have the energy of a golden retriever. Today you've seemed more like a geriatric basset hound, long face and all."

I give a short laugh. "Golden retriever? I guess I'll take that as a compliment."

"Hey, I love gold retrievers." Pete smiles at me kindly, and I relent.

"Drew broke up with me."

"What?" Pete looks gratifyingly shocked.

"I know! It came out of nowhere. One minute we were talking about Hot Brew, the next he was saying he was moving back to L.A. Apparently, he still has an apartment there. I thought he was really making an effort to settle in Rosedale. But he said we can't make decisions about our futures based on the last few weeks, which totally threw me. I mean, I guess it's a little fast, but I thought maybe after this weekend I'd talk to him about giving notice at my job, moving out of New York."

"After this weekend?"

"I have to pull off this event," I say. "It's everything I've been working toward for months—almost a year."

"Well, maybe you should have brought up some of this stuff a little sooner. It sounds like he doesn't know you were thinking about those things." Pete doesn't tell me I'm way off base in thinking about quitting my job and moving to Rosedale, but now that I hear it coming out of my mouth, I wonder if maybe I am getting ahead of myself.

Maybe Drew's right.

Maybe this isn't the grand love affair I thought it was.

But when I imagine going back to my cramped apartment, just me and my bicycle in the Big Apple, no Drew, no Cinnamon, no running into friends on the street, going to a job that offers little more than a paycheck—I didn't work so hard to keep going after Brock died just to live that way.

I want what Drew and I were starting to build here. I want the cozy downtown and the challenge of bringing a bike shop here. Maybe I'd have to do some marketing work on the side for a while, but that would be okay. Rent in Rosedale couldn't possibly be higher than what I'm paying now.

I can move here, I can start over—again. The only problem is that it won't mean as much without Drew.

But Pete's right. I never actually told Drew any of my thoughts about the future. As far as he knows, after the bike event, I'm heading back to the city.

"I need to talk to him," I say as Pete sets a steaming mug in front of me.

"You need to talk to him," Pete agrees.

"Do you think I'm making a mistake to turn my life upside down after a few weeks?"

"You love him, right?"

I could kiss Pete for seeing this for what it is.

"I love him."

"Then no. I've been there, well—Jack's the one who knew first. We made it hard for a second, but it was so easy once we let ourselves feel what we were feeling. And you know what you feel for him. The question is, what does he feel for you?"

"I don't know." I know we've both talked around our feelings, but even as scared as I've been to push him too far, too fast, we've both met each other where we are. He's been with me every step of the way until today. So if I love him, maybe he loves me too.

God, I hope so.

"So what are you still doing here? Go talk to your man," Pete says.

I hug Pete, take a gulp of my still-too-hot tea and burn my tongue, but I barely feel it in my haste to gather my stuff and my bike and get on the road.

It's been hours since Drew left for Hot Brew, but since he doesn't pick up when I call him, I figure it's the best place to start. I pull up just as Meadow is locking the front door.

"Meadow, hey. Do you happen to know where Drew went after he left here?"

She shakes her head. "Sorry, Charlie. I didn't see Drew today."

"Really? He told me he was coming here. It would have been around one?"

"I've been here all day, and he didn't come in. Everything okay?"

"Don't worry about it," I say more calmly than I feel. "He's probably home."

But when I reach the end of the driveway about

fifteen minutes later, his car isn't parked in its spot. Cinnamon is sitting in the window, and I wave at him. He flicks his tail at me. I'm partially relieved. Drew wouldn't have left without making arrangements for Cinnamon.

But where is he?

I force myself to breathe. This is not Brock being there one moment, gone the next. This isn't my dad abandoning his responsibilities because he got tired of the life he'd built. Even if Drew doesn't love me back, he's not intentionally trying to hurt me.

I repeat that like a mantra as I go to my place, unlock the door, bring my bike inside. The chill is back, so I bump up the heat and take a hot shower. Dressed again, I check my phone and the parking spot. Nothing.

Maybe he really did leave me for good.

BY THE TIME the credits roll on the monster movie, my tongue feels like it's been abraded by a salt lick. The bag of popcorn is empty and I'm dying for water. I stumble out to the lobby, experiencing the disorientation of going from the dark theater to finding it's still light outside.

I slake my thirst at the drinking fountain, reluctantly check my phone. Alyson left a thumbs up to my message about Phoebe's notes.

Nothing from Charlie, not that I expected anything.

I was sort of hoping that after the movie, I'd discover my earlier conversation with Charlie had all been in my head. That I hadn't actually overreacted to the situation and not only broken up with him, but told him I was selling my house and moving back to L.A.

I don't want to sell my house.

I don't want to move back to L.A.

And I don't want to break up with the man I've fallen in love with.

Oh fuck.

What have I done?

If I'm this messed up, how is Charlie feeling right now? Some of the things I said—he hadn't fought me, just seemed...sad.

I knew that Charlie was more vulnerable than he seemed. I knew how hard it was for him to keep going, to move on and thrive after Brock's death.

I knew how much it hurt him every time someone left him, teenage me probably included, even if that wasn't my fault.

And then I went and did the thing all over again, because I was scared he didn't want me for keeps.

But what if he does?

It's not that we have to be together twenty-four-seven forever. But if I want to be in a relationship with him, I need to be in the relationship with him, not go running away.

It's so simple...but somehow it hasn't been easy.

Even if I tell him what I want, I have to be prepared to accept that he might not want the same things. But I have to be honest with him, and with myself. I know I want to make a real go of it in Rosedale, which means I need to live in Rosedale. And if he doesn't, well, New York isn't that far away. I have a car, and there's a train that runs from Rosedale to the city. The same train that brought Charlie to me in the first place.

Long distance would be a hell of a lot better than never seeing him again.

Only how can I make up for being such a dolt today?

If there's one thing I've learned from movies, it's that there's got to be a grand gesture when the romantic lead screws up. And even though my head is swimming from eating popcorn for lunch, and I'm still thirsty, and my eyes feel itchy as if I've been crying for hours even though I haven't shed a single tear, I know what I can do to start making things right.

I get out my phone and call Alyson. She picks up on the second ring.

"I started pulling the tracks for the music cues Phoebe wants," she says.

"That's great. But I actually want you to stop working."

"Huh?"

"I want you to come to Rosedale for the bike event on Saturday. I'll pay for your ticket, and I'll get you a car from the airport so you don't have to take the train."

"Isn't that like a three-hour ride? It'll cost a fortune. Not to mention the price of a last-minute plane ticket."

"I don't care. You should be here. It'll be a great surprise for Charlie. Please say you'll come. Get a ticket right now."

"Okay. I would love to see you guys. Is everything okay?"

"I kind of messed up and broke up with him."

I hold the phone away from my ear as the expected high-pitched noise ensues. "Drew!" she admonishes me with a single syllable.

"But I'm trying to fix it."

"By offering me up as a grand gesture?" She's a film nerd, too.

"Exactly."

"Well, I guess it's a good idea," she says grumpily.

"Besides, if this doesn't work, at least I'll be on hand to try to salvage things myself."

"I hope it doesn't come to that." But it's nice to know she's still rooting for us, no matter what bad choices I made.

"Okay, I'll find a flight and text you the details."

"I'll get you a place to stay, and, oh, can you do me another favor?"

She lets out a long-suffering sigh. "I suppose."

I tell her what I need, and she actually laughs. "Okay, that's a good idea. I'll do it."

"Thanks, Alyson. See you soon."

"Exciting! Okay!"

"Oh, and obviously, don't tell Charlie. That'll ruin the surprise."

"My lips are sealed. But you should try to make up with him even before I get there."

"I'll try."

The next person I call is Jack, but he doesn't answer. I leave a brief message asking him to return my call.

Then Charlie calls me, and I panic and stare down at the phone. I haven't figured out what to say to him yet. If I answer, I could make things worse. But if I don't answer, I could lose my chance to talk to him at all. I go to accept his call, but I'm too late. I've missed him.

I look around in despair. I'm still in the lobby of the little movie theater, and I probably look like a lunatic.

I'm also a little dizzy. I guess protein is a priority. Then finding Charlie and begging him to give me another chance.

TWENTY-EIGHT
CHARLIE

IT'S ALMOST ENTIRELY dark outside, making the headlights sweeping up the driveway easy to spot through the guest house front windows. Drew's back. I grab a hoodie and rush out to meet him. Maybe he doesn't want to talk to me, but I let him talk plenty earlier today—now it's my turn.

But when I get to the front of the main house, I see a plumber's van instead of Drew's sedan. A vaguely familiar young guy gets out of the driver's side.

"Hi," he says. "Sorry, I'm later than I thought. Is Drew here?"

"No. I'm Charlie. I'm staying in his guest house."

"Name's Lucas. I'm here to look at the heat. You think it's okay if I go in?"

"Let me see if it's open." I try the front door, but it's locked. My key only works on the guest house door. But the back door might be open.

"Hang on." I jog around the side of the house. Drew's bike still rests near the back door, where we left it after our last ride together, only a couple of days ago. I try the knob—it's unlocked, so I let myself in, turning on lights as I walk through to the front and let Lucas in.

I left my phone in the guest house, so I can't text Drew to see if this is okay, but since the house feels stone cold, I don't think he'll mind.

"You know where to go?" I ask the repairman.

"Oh yeah, I'm familiar with this system. I keep telling Drew he's gotta upgrade. Maybe this'll be the thing that does it."

"Maybe." Lucas disappears down the basement stairs. I'm sure it's fine to leave him to run and get my phone. Cinnamon pads over as I'm deciding whether to go from the front or the back. He head-butts my shin repeatedly until I pick him up and he starts purring in my arms.

"What's up, buddy?" I ask. "You hungry for dinner?" It's so unlike Drew to not be here to meet Lucas, or to forget about Cinnamon.

I set aside my unease and pour some kibble into Cinnamon's dish. I know Drew gives him a dollop of wet food at night, too. There's an open can in the fridge, so I add the contents to Cinnamon's meal. I rinse out the can and put it in the recycle bin. I know how to do all of these things because I've been a part of Drew's life these last few weeks. I can't believe he's throwing all of that away.

For the first time, I let myself truly feel the weight of his absence. I'm here in his kitchen, where we've shared so much of ourselves, of our lives. To have that suddenly gone hurts. A lot.

Headlights pierce through the kitchen window. This

time it's clearly Drew's car, which he parks next to the van. He comes running to the front door. I stay put while he lets himself in. When I hear the door close, I call out, "In the kitchen."

His steps slow as he nears the kitchen door, but then he's there, swallowed up by the oversized sweater he's apparently been wearing all day over his shapeless jeans and his sneakers. He hasn't changed, but the sight of him makes my heart ache more than I thought it would.

"Charlie. You're here."

"I let Lucas in. I hope that's okay."

"Thanks for that."

"I also fed your cat," I add acerbically.

He winces. "Thanks. It got late all of a sudden."

"Where—" I stop. It's none of my business where he's been all day. I take a breath. I want to say my piece, but I'm paralyzed by conflicting emotions. I want to hug him. I want to yell at him. I don't know where to start.

"I'm glad you're here," he says, filling the silence. "I'm sorry I missed your call. Are you okay?"

I glare at him. "Am I okay? Am I *okay*?" My voice rises with the repetition and Cinnamon looks up from his food in alarm. "You broke up with me," I manage to get out without breaking down. "No, I am not okay."

"I'm sorry," he says, taking a step toward me. It's my turn to shrink away from him. I edge back, bump into the counter.

"You said a lot of things earlier today. I need to say a few things, too, because maybe I haven't been clear. After I say these things, you're either going to want to reconsider, or you're going to think I'm nuts and run for the hills. But since you were going to do that second thing anyway, I don't have much to lose." He opens his mouth, but I put up a hand. "No, please, let me just get this out. Okay?"

He shuts his mouth.

"Okay. I realize I've been very focused on this bike event. It's been a huge deal for me for months, and it's finally happening, so I haven't had time for other things, like talking about us, and for that I'm sorry." Drew opens his mouth again and I glare at him. His mouth closes and I continue, "So I might have forgotten to mention some stuff I've been thinking about lately. Like how I want to put in notice at my job. I'm sick of the city. I hate my apartment. Jack was right—he told me it was only a matter of time before the people he loves all move here. Well, my time is now. I'm ready to become a Rosedalian."

One corner of Drew's mouth lifts up at that, but I can't be encouraged by his response to our in-joke. "I was thinking you'd be here, too, but that's up to you. Either way, I love it here. For too long, my life has been about keeping my head above water. But now I'm ready to truly move forward, to start building something more, to focus on my future. I don't entirely know what that's going to look like, where I'll live, or what I'll do, but I'm excited to figure it out, even if I have to do it by myself."

I pause, but he keeps his mouth shut. He can be taught.

"Finally, I know it's none of my business what you do with this house, or your life. You have every right to live wherever you choose. But you deserve to have an amazing life, so I just hope you don't make your choice based on fear, but out of hope. Out of love, even," I add, my voice dropping. Here goes nothing. "Speaking of which, you should know that I love you."

I can't mistake the way Drew's eyes widen at that, but since I can't interpret that response, I barrel on. "It's fast, but who cares? We've had a connection since high school. I've always been attracted to you, both to your body and your soul. I think you've felt it, too. So yeah. I wanted you to know."

I've said pretty much what I wanted to say, and the fight's gone out of me. Sure, Drew hurt me earlier with his seemingly cavalier tossing aside of what we had. But I've been honest with him, and I'm at peace with that.

He looks at me, his eyes still wide. His mouth still closed.

"You can talk now," I say.

"Thank you," he says immediately. "I have way more to say than this, but I'll just start with the big one. I love you, too."

It feels like the sun's come out, right there in Drew's kitchen. "You do?"

"Yes, Charlie Linden. I'm in love with you. And I've never said that to anyone before. Am I doing it right?"

"Is your heart racing? Are your palms sweaty? Do you feel a little bit like you might throw up?"

"Check. Check. And check," he answers.

"Then yep, you're doing it right." I laugh, giddy with relief and happiness, and we meet in the center of the room, our mouths finding each other instinctively. My arms clamp around him, so tight he can't hug me back, and he lets me kiss the breath out of him.

"God, I was so scared you weren't coming back," I say, voicing my fear out loud for the first time.

"I'm so sorry I did that to you," he says. "I was just at the movies. Trying to escape my own bad decisions."

"The movies." That sounds like Drew. "I'm glad you came back."

"I'll always come back," he says, and I tighten my grip on him, as if I can protect him from anything in this world that might prevent him from keeping his promise.

"I love you," I whisper against his mouth.

"I can't believe it." He smiles. "But I'm so happy you do."

Someone clears their throat just outside the kitchen door, and I peer over Drew's shoulder.

Lucas shuffles from foot to foot at the doorway, rubbing the back of his neck. "Uh, sorry to interrupt, but I got the heat going again, for now."

The kitchen does feel incrementally warmer now that he mentions it, though it could be my flush of happiness at having my feelings returned, not to mention the proximity of the beautiful man in my arms.

"Lucas, so sorry, I forgot all about you," Drew says, gently disentangling himself from me while staying close. "What do I owe you?"

"You know what, if you let me order that new tankless unit, I'll throw in today's visit for free. It's either that, or you're going to be seeing me a lot more this winter."

Drew glances at me. "Well, makes sense to upgrade if I'm going to be living here, right?"

"You'll need heat to get through the winter, for sure. I

don't think we can generate enough, just the two of us," I joke.

"We could try," he says.

Lucas's cheeks are flaming red, and he starts to back down the hallway. "Just let me know soon, okay?"

Drew laughs. "I'll take it. Order away."

Lucas pauses, grins. "Really? So you're sticking around Rosedale?"

Drew looks at me. I've never seen him smiling this hard. "Most definitely. Call me the newest Rosedalian."

"SO, did we just decide you were going to move in with me?" I ask as we climb the stairs to my—our?—room a while later.

"Uh, well, I don't want to impose. I could find some-place in town, maybe—"

"Charlie, stop. I want you to move in with me," I say. We're good at talking around each other, but the knowl-edge that this isn't just a passing fling makes me more assertive. "I like having you here."

"In that case, I accept," he says immediately. "Should be interesting. I haven't had a roommate since I was in college."

"Were you sleeping with them?" I ask as I turn down the sheets on the bed. The room is cool, but the radiators are working again to warm the air.

"No," he says, toeing off his sneakers. "My last room-mate was a very straight business major."

"Then it's not the same. We're not going to be roommates; we're going to be cohabitating boyfriends." I shed my sweater, kick off my shoes.

"I think I see the difference," he says, pulling his long-sleeved tee over his head to reveal his torso. "When we fight about the dishes and the laundry, we can have sex afterward."

"Exactly." I tackle him onto the bed, and he goes willingly, shifting around until we're slotted together, chest to chest, hip to hip.

Charlie's face is so close I can see the fine lines beginning to radiate from the corners of his eyes. We're getting older. I'm going to get the privilege of watching Charlie Linden age. I'm so lucky.

His gaze slides away from me under my scrutiny. "You don't think we're moving too fast? Before you said we shouldn't make decisions based on a few weeks of hooking up."

My stomach dives. "I shouldn't have—first of all, we weren't just hooking up. I can't believe I said that. I was scared that this didn't mean to you what it meant to me, and I was just trying to—"

"Protect yourself," he finishes. "I get it. But it still hurt."

"I know." I lift my chin and kiss his forehead. "I'll never do that again."

"We're probably going to mess up and hurt each other once in a while," he says, smiling sadly. "I just hope we can stay and talk about it. Okay?"

"Okay." I kiss him again, on his mouth this time, then once more for good measure. "By the way, I think you're right that I need to talk to a professional about my dad. It's overdue."

"I think it might really help," Charlie says. "Let me know if you need advice on finding someone."

"Thanks. And to answer your original question, no, I don't think we're moving too fast. All we really have is right now, right?"

He swallows, and he closes his eyes for a long moment. When he opens them, they look a little wet. "Right."

I know he's thinking about Brock, about time running out. I'm thinking about my dad, too, and how you can't count on being given endless chances. But Charlie and I have one big chance to hold on to what we have together. "I want to be with you, Charlie, right here, right now. But I also want to build something with you—I want to trust that there's going to be a future for us. I want to enjoy the moment and plan for all the moments ahead. Can we do both?"

"Yes," he says, and then he kisses me, and it feels like a promise. Like we're in this together, finally, instead of two individual lonely people stumbling around in the dark. We found each other, and we're stumbling into the light.

We've gone from long-lost friends to lovers to partners in the space of a few weeks, but I'm ready to trust that we know what we want at this stage of our lives. I've spent too much time being wishy-washy—maybe I was afraid I didn't have the inner strength to stick to a commitment. But now that I've acknowledged what I want, it seems like the easiest thing in the world to take it.

I want this house. I want Rosedale. I want a community. I want Charlie.

And Charlie wants me.

I deepen the kiss, needing to show him how very, very much I want him. He lets me press him into the mattress, suck his bottom lip into my mouth and fatten it up. I lick his tongue—he groans and opens up wider for me. Every button I try pushing seems to work on him. Everything I ask for, he's willing to give me, plus more. He wraps his strong thighs around me, locking me into place as he rolls his hips, rubbing our cocks together through my jeans and his joggers.

It feels so good to let myself go, to not be afraid to show myself to him, to be messy and silly and dorky and, yes, a little dominant. A little sweet, too.

I marvel at how well-matched we are. From the first moment I kissed him, he let me; he encouraged me. No, before that, when we were clueless teenagers who didn't know how to communicate what we were feeling, but still experiencing a pull toward each other that was real, that stayed with us over the years and over the miles.

But we're not teenagers now. We know what to do, how to make each other feel good. And it's my personal challenge to make Charlie feel as good as humanly possible as many times as I possibly can.

"What do you want?" I ask.

"You," he answers simply. My heart hurts with how much I love him, with how deep this runs.

I kiss him hard and fierce. He seems to understand and kisses me back just as hard, and then there's no more talking, just mouths on skin, hands removing clothes.

We've had sex a dozen times in this bed, but this is the first time I know we're making love.

I get out the lube and a condom, then roll onto my back and spread my legs. The other day when he opened me up and finished with his cock partially inside me—it was so hot, so intense that I almost blacked out. I never particularly enjoyed bottoming with the other guys I've tried it with, but I know Charlie's going to make it good.

"I want you to fuck me. Can you do the prep?"

He nods, expression focused, his nimble fingers opening me slowly, but confidently, until I'm taking three. It feels full and intense again, but not as overwhelming as the first time. Now I just have this persistent ache, a need to feel Charlie inside me, a need to give myself entirely over to him since he's so very good at doing the same for me.

I've been stroking myself lazily while he works, flicking my thumb over the head of my cock, damp with pre-come. "I think I'm ready," I say.

Charlie kisses me, wipes his hand on a tissue. "I think you should be on top. It'll give you more control."

"I trust you," I say, because it's true. "Let's try this first, okay?"

"Okay. But you just say stop and I'll stop."

"I know."

He gets the condom on, slicks himself up. His cock looks bigger tonight for some reason, but it's got to be an optical illusion. More lube gets drizzled on my hole, and the area around it, than seems strictly necessary, but I appreciate him playing it safe. I can feel the lube seeping up my crack, wetting the small of my back. We're going to have to change the sheets again before we go to sleep, and I make a mental note to order another couple of sets.

"What are you thinking about?" Charlie asks, the tip of his cock resting on my hole, but not pushing in.

"Um, I was thinking about ordering more sheets."

He leans back on his heels. "Hell no. I'm not doing this right if you're thinking about online shopping."

"No! I was just thinking about how messy they're getting. Please don't stop."

"Please get on top, babe. You'll like it better."

"Fine." We renegotiate the space, and at this point I'm so impatient to have him inside me that I just sit on his cock, taking him in one smooth motion.

"Holy hell, babe," he grunts, holding onto my hips. "Are you okay?"

"Oh yeah," I say with a moan. "I'm so fucking okay." I'm fucking full, and he's done such a good job of prepping me that I'm not even feeling a burn, just the stretch and the slide as I experimentally rise up an inch, then sit back down.

"More lube?" he asks anxiously.

"No, this is perfect." I sigh and rise up two inches this time. Yeah, he was right. I like being in control. I fold myself over, cataloging every new twinge and ache, my cock seeming to respond to every single one, and kiss him sloppily on the mouth. My hands stroke down his shoulders and arms, then I pin him to the bed and start to rock up and down in earnest. He's inside me, but it's like I'm fucking him, slowly, thoroughly, at my pace and at my discretion.

"Yeah..." He moans when I squeeze his arms and

slam back down on him. "Use my cock to feel good, babe."

I do exactly that, squeezing his arms once, knowing he'll keep them where they are so I can sit up, strip my own cock in time to the bounce, feeling so full, so over-stimulated, that the sight of him lying on the bed, eyes black, smooth, muscular body rigid beneath me, is enough to almost send me over the edge. I pull back just in time, squeezing the base of my cock to give me a reprieve. "You look so good, Charlie. I love you so much."

He moans the loudest I've ever heard him, a wail he can't stop, and then his hips are stuttering upward, driving his cock even deeper into me. "I'm coming, babe," he says, telling me something I already know. "Holy hell, I'm coming."

"Yeah, Charlie." I tighten my knees at his hips, go back to jacking my cock, letting myself feel everything, letting the orgasm rush through me, feeling it in my ass and my balls and my cock. Watching him get painted with my come.

I disengage us a minute later, feeling it a little more than I expected as he leaves me entirely. It's the best time I've ever had receiving, but it's still a lot of work. We clean each other up minimally and briefly brush our teeth, the lure of sleep reeling us in after our emotional roller coaster of a day.

"I'm so—" Charlie yawns so wide I can hear his jaw crack. "—tired."

"You need a good night's sleep. You've got a couple of big days coming up."

He pulls on an old T-shirt of mine that he's been using to sleep in lately. "Don't I know it."

"But it's going to be fabulous. And I'll be there for whatever you need." It was so sucky of me to tell him I wouldn't attend.

"Anything?" He smiles sleepily at me and nestles his head on a pillow. I flick off the light, make sure my phone alarm is set to wake us up early, but not too early.

"Sure. Coffee runs, holding signs, blow jobs."

"I don't think there will be much time for blow jobs in between the other activities, but your offer is noted."

"What about a little videography?" I ask. I don't know why the idea didn't occur to me earlier. "I can record footage of the event and cut together a little video afterward."

He opens his eyes at that. "Really?"

"Sure. It would be a nice commemoration of the first annual Brock Harris Memorial Bike Ride for Lyme Disease Awareness and Prevention."

"First annual?"

"It's going to be such a success you'll have to do it again next year."

"Whatever you say, babe." He closes his eyes again. "And yes, I'd love for you to take some video and put something together."

"On it," I say, already mentally pulling together a to-do list.

"And maybe a blow job after?" he asks hopefully.

I kiss his temple, settle into my own pillow, and pull the quilt over our shoulders. "And maybe a blow job after."

THIRTY

CHARLIE

I COULDN'T HAVE ORDERED a nicer day for Brock's memorial ride. The sun came out to dispel the October morning chill and warm the backs of the hundred-plus cyclists in the ten-mile ride. I'm among them, the event going well enough that I think I can risk stepping away from the organizational end of things to participate on my bike.

Everyone's stepped up beautifully and done their part. Jack and Pete helped me transport and set up everything for the volunteers, who've been eating cookies from Beck's Cookie Counter and drinking coffee from Hot Brew in record volume, but also directing parking, traffic, riders, setting up signs and water stations, and answering questions. I've barely seen Drew, but that's okay. He kissed me goodbye this morning and told me it was going to go great.

So far, so good.

The few times I've spotted Drew, he's been looking

through the viewfinder of the digital camera he's using to document the day. I know he's not an expert videographer, but I'm sure whatever he's capturing will be nice to have later, when I can slow down and actually absorb everything that happened.

I've already seen Brock's parents, who hugged me tight and didn't fuss too much when they saw me wipe away a tear. My mom's here, too. It's only about an hour and a half drive from her home in West Hartford, so she came up for the day and has been hanging out at the volunteer table, eating her share of the cookies.

The ride isn't a race, but I keep to the front of the pack to make sure everything's okay with the route. I breathe deep as I push myself up the first hill and try to focus on why we're all here. Because Brock isn't here, and he should be, and I'm never, ever going to forget him.

I miss him so much, but I don't feel angry anymore at having to go on without him. Instead, I'm grateful for the chance to know him, grateful for the time we shared. Grateful to whatever's pulling our strings around the universe for bringing Drew's and my strings together again. Of course, according to Allie, that would be her. I'm willing to give her partial credit.

The end of the ride comes up all too quickly, the miles having disappeared beneath my tires. We're finishing at the end of Main Street, where there's a parking lot and a little green space. A crowd has gathered to cheer us on as we pass the final marker, and I do a double take when I see a short, round woman in the crowd. She's got brown hair streaked with magenta and hexagonal glasses. It's my sister, waving at me and jumping up and down, all while holding some kind of large lumpy package.

I whoop and bring my bike to a stop in front of her, making sure I'm not going to be blocking any of the riders behind me. "What are you doing here?"

She throws the arm not holding the package around my shoulders and hugs me. "Drew made me come at the last minute. He wanted me to be here."

"I'm so glad you are. How did you get here?"

"I actually arrived late last night. I'm staying at Jack and Pete's. They have the cutest dog. Maybe I should get a dog, since the dating thing isn't working out that well."

"You could get a dog," I say, "but you have time, Allie."

"Ugh. I hate that name, Charles." She sticks her tongue out at me. "Oh, this is for you. It's also from Drew. I think he was worried you wouldn't forgive him for being a dumbass or whatever went down between you two, even though I knew you would because you are a softie and the two of you are supposed to be together. Here."

She pushes the package at me, and I try to juggle it without letting my bike fall to the ground. "Uh. Can this wait?"

"Charlie! Look who I found." It's my mom, walking up arm in arm with—

"Paloma! Oh my god, you're here, too?" I had no idea she was going to be in town for this.

"I decided to come and see the miracle of you and Drew Hersh for myself. Oh, and contribute to the cause, of course."

I get a hug from my friend, who smells like jasmine, while my mom exclaims and forces Allie into another big hug.

"You didn't bring Seb?"

"He had to work, but he says hi. And that if you need a best man, he calls dibs."

"Paloma, god, chill," I say. "We're only moving in together, not getting married."

Three women speak simultaneously. "You're moving in together?"

"Uh, yeah."

Everyone starts talking at once, incomprehensibly, but I think the gist is they are excited for me—for us.

"Where is your beau?" My mom is a young fifty-five, but she reads a lot of historical romance.

"He's around here somewhere, taking video of the event. Speaking of which, I have to get the first race going. I'll see all of you later, okay?"

I steer over to the race route, belatedly realizing I'm still holding the mysterious package that Drew gave me by way of Allie. I tear off the paper to reveal a giant red gummy bear wrapped in cellophane. Its empty eyes stare at me. I laugh until my sides hurt.

Drew

I've gotten decent footage of the day's setup, Charlie's heartfelt opening remarks, and the start of the ten-mile ride. Next is getting over to the end of the route to capture the riders coming home. But first, I need a refill of my coffee at the volunteer station. I find Meadow there, filling the urn with a fresh brew. It's piping hot when it goes into my travel mug, and I sigh appreciatively.

"Are you racing today?" I ask Meadow.

"No, but Melissa will. She's been training all week."

"Nice."

"I'm also not racing," Beck offers. He's restocking the snack table with more Brock's Banana Split cookies. I already had one, but could it really hurt to take a second? It's a special day, after all. "But my better half is. He already had a bike, and I still need to get one."

"Too bad there isn't a bike shop in Rosedale, huh?" I say.

"Oh my gosh, there totally needs to be," Beck says.

"And your boy needs to open it," Jack says, strolling up and swiping a cookie, Pete right beside him. "Beck can help if he needs pointers on launching a business in Rosedale. I can give him some capital if he wants it."

"Don't you think you should bask in your triumph of bringing two more people into the Rosedale fold before you try to push your friend into a new business venture?" Pete asks, stealing a bite of Jack's cookie.

"Oh, I'm taking all the credit for that, for sure," Jack says.

I laugh. "So you're the reason we're becoming official Rosedalians."

"Rosedalians—I like it. And I suggested that Charlie hold this event here, so yeah, I'm taking credit for everything, including the two of you getting together."

"You'll have to share some of the glory with Alyson. Thanks for giving her a place to stay, by the way."

"No problem. She's a hoot and we have lots of room."

"She can bunk with us starting tonight. I just wanted it to be a surprise for today. Oh shoot, the riders are starting to come back." I hoist my camera, check the battery level; I'm good to go.

I quickly trot down the block, taking some still photos on my phone, then find the corner I scouted earlier with an out-of-the-way vantage point of the returning riders. I raise the camera and start recording. Charlie's one of the earliest to show up, of course. I track him to the crowd cheering them on, and grin when I see through the viewfinder that he's spotted Alyson. I wanted them to have their moment, but it's cool to see how obviously stunned and excited he is to see her, even from a distance. Then an older woman approaches them, arms linked with a younger woman with long dark hair, and I realize it's Paloma with someone who must be Charlie's mom, neither of whom I've seen in person in fifteen years. There are hugs all around. I didn't know Paloma was coming—she must have planned her own surprise visit.

I hang back, not wanting to intrude on the mini reunion. Besides, I have a job to do, and I swing the camera back over to the cyclists, finishing the ride in clumps of twos and threes.

When it seems as if most everyone has made it back, it's time for the heats to begin. There are several age brackets that will be racing on surface streets that the Rosedale Police Department has already closed to vehicle traffic.

I make my way through the crowd to the starting line, where the first heat will depart from in a few minutes.

Charlie is talking to one of the Rosedale police officers who has been working the event, nodding along to something he says. They shake hands, then Charlie turns his attention to a volunteer who seems to have a question for him. He's in his element, his energy never flagging. He's amazing.

He catches sight of me after the volunteer heads off. "Babe." He waves me over.

"Hey, looks like everything is going well."

"I can't believe you brought Allie here," he says, wagging a finger at me. "You little sneak."

"I wanted an ace in the hole," I say. "And also she should be here."

"And the freaking enormous gummy bear? Which is safely with my mother, who you need to say hello to, by the way."

"A second ace in the hole?" I sigh. "I just—I didn't know how to fix the mess I made, so I had some contingency plans. But it turns out I didn't need them because you are the most forgiving man in the world and happen to love me back."

"You don't need to fly my relatives across the country and buy me presents to show me you care about me," he says, "though I'm glad you did. All you have to do is look at me and I can tell. You're crazy about me."

"Look at you like this?" I stare intently into his eyes, the eyes of the man I love more than anything on this planet.

"Yeah, like that." Charlie stares back at me, and it's

cheesy, but I can see the love in his eyes, just like he can no doubt see the love in mine.

We break at the same time, giggling at our corniness. And then I kiss him, and I could live in this moment for the rest of my life.

EPILOGUE
CHARLIE

Three months later

"IT'S ABSOLUTELY PERFECT. Don't you think it's perfect?" Drew asks as we walk around the space. We're viewing an empty store on Linden Street, just off Main.

"This building is extra deep, so you could set up a repair area in the back," Noelle, the real estate agent Jack recommended to me, says. "Let's check it out."

I follow her and Drew down a short hallway to the back rooms of the space. One room could easily be turned into a workshop for bike tune-ups and repairs, the other could be used to store inventory. There's a bathroom, and even a little room that could be an office. This is all so ideal it's scary.

"The owners are willing to offer the first month rent-free, but I think we should negotiate a lower overall rent. This unit has been vacant long enough that I think they might work with us on the price," Noelle says authoritatively. "We could draft a proposal and have it over to them later today."

My stomach gives an unwelcome lurch. "Um. I think I need a minute, sorry," I say. I speed walk out the front door, randomly make a left. It's January, it's freezing, and Drew took my puffy winter jacket when we went inside the empty store, so now I'm cold. Instead of turning around and apologizing, I dart into the store next door. It's warm as a tropical island in here, and it smells fantastic. Living things, or what were once living things, cover almost every surface—houseplants in colorful pots, cut flowers in vases waiting to be turned into bouquets or arrangements, dried flowers hanging from the rafters that give off a papery odor. I've walked into a florist's shop.

"Can I help you?" A tall, thin man with long, almost white blond hair comes out from behind a cluttered countertop. He wipes his hands on a denim work apron.

"Um. I'm not actually in the market for flowers," I say, though maybe buying Drew something to convey that I'm sorry for bailing on him and Noelle is in order. "I was just looking for a temporary escape."

"Oh, well, this is a good place for that," he says. "Mind if I ask what you're escaping from? Do I need to call the cops or something?"

I laugh and shake my head. "No, nothing like that. I was touring the space next door, and I got a little panicky."

"Oh?" He looks at me with more interest. "What's your business?" Of course, he'd be curious about a potential new neighbor.

"I'm thinking of opening up a bike shop. Bike sales, repairs, that kind of thing."

"A bike shop?" He puts his chin in his hand. "Well, that's something Rosedale needs," he says finally. "I approve."

"So does everyone else. And I want to do it, truly. But now that it's actually happening—I'm just a little nervous, I guess."

"Totally understandable. Hey—you're the one who organized the bike thing this fall, aren't you?"

"Yep," I confirm. "Charlie Linden."

"I'm Shay Brierley," he says. "And this is Linden Street. It's a sign."

"Yeah. When we found out this place was available, Drew, my boyfriend, said I could name the shop Linden Street Bikes."

"I love it." He narrows his pale eyes. "But you don't?"

"I do love it, actually. It's just—"

"Charlie, there you are." Drew comes in with a concerned look on his face, bringing a draft of frigid January air with him. Noelle is nowhere to be seen.

"Sorry, babe." I give him a guilty smile. He's been nothing but supportive and I'm being a baby.

He drapes my jacket over my shoulders, squeezes them lightly. "It's okay. I told Noelle we'd get back to her later."

"Was she mad?"

"She was fine. She knows this is a big step." He looks at Shay. "Hi. Sorry—am I interrupting you?"

"Of course not," I say. "Drew, this is Shay, Shay, this is Drew."

They wave at each other.

"You want to get going? We can go to Hot Brew, talk over some peppermint hot chocolate," he suggests.

"Sure. Sorry to crash in here," I say to Shay. "I'll, uh, I'll definitely be back the next time I need flowers."

"You never buy me flowers," Drew says, laughing.

"Maybe I should."

"You definitely should. Everyone should get flowers at least once in a while," Shay says. "And I'm not only saying that because my livelihood depends on it."

"Then let's get some now," I say, turning to Drew. "What do you want?"

"Um. What do you suggest?" he asks Shay in turn.

"Most of the cut flowers we have right now are flown in from South America—roses, lilies, the usual. If you want something living that'll still be green in a few months, how about a peperomia? It needs a sunny spot by a window, and let the soil dry out between waterings. In the spring, you can keep it inside or put it outside, just not in super harsh direct sunlight."

"Is it okay for cats? I've heard some houseplants are bad for them," Drew says.

"Great question. It's totally pet-friendly."

"Sold."

I hand over my credit card, and while Shay's bustling around selecting a peperomia for us to adopt, I lean my head on Drew's shoulder. "I really am sorry about that. I know this is the right thing to do. It just got really real for a second. And I still have a hard time believing it's not all going to disappear."

"I know what you mean," he says. "I've been feeling

that way since you rode up my driveway last fall. That this is a dream I'm going to wake up from. But it's not."

"Not a dream?"

"It's a dream come true," he says. "It's better than a dream, because even if it isn't perfect—even if we're not perfect—"

"Well, I'm definitely not," I break in.

"I'm not so sure about that," he says with a smile. "You're definitely perfect for me. But even if we're not perfect, and the shop fails, and you have to go back to some boring marketing job—"

"Wow, I thought you were trying to make me feel better."

"—even if all those things happen, we still have right this very minute, don't we? You and me, together. I can't ask for anything more than that."

"How about a plant?" Shay says, presenting us with a beautiful potted peperomia.

"Our first plant child," I say.

"Relationship milestone," Drew says.

"Thanks, Shay. We'll be back."

"I hope so, neighbor," he says with a wink.

Out on the street, Drew holds the plant while I put my jacket on all the way. "We better skip Hot Brew, go home, and get this inside."

"And then you can get inside me," Drew says with a comical leer.

I laugh. "Now you're talking. And then I'll call Noelle and tell her to put the paperwork together." I take a breath, and I don't feel like throwing up. Progress.

"Really?" Drew sounds surprised, but happy.

"Really. Linden Street Bikes is going to be a thing."

"It's going to be an incredible thing," Drew says as we walk to his car. It now has Connecticut plates, because he's an official Rosedalian now.

And so am I.

"Let's go home."

And we do.

Thank you for reading *Autumn Crush*! Missed Beck and Donovan's story? Catch up with *Cool for the Summer*, then read all about Shay Brierley and his plans for the plant shop, as well as his new neighbor, Connor, in the next Rosedale romance, *Winter Under the Covers*.

For more information on Lyme disease and how to prevent it, visit the CDC website at cdc.gov. Stay safe!

Keep reading to get the recipe for Brock's Banana Split cookies.

Happy reading and happy eating!

xoxo,

Elle

BROCK'S BANANA SPLIT COOKIES RECIPE

Ingredients

½ cup room-temperature unsalted butter

¾ cup chunky non-natural peanut butter

1 cup lightly packed light brown sugar

1 tablespoon vanilla extract

1 large egg

1 egg yolk

1 medium to large ripe banana, mashed

2 cups all purpose flour

1 teaspoon baking powder

½ teaspoon baking soda

1 teaspoon salt

1 cup peanut butter chips

1 cup dark chocolate chips

Optional: chopped peanuts, rainbow sprinkles

Instructions

Preheat oven to 425 degrees F. Line two baking sheets with parchment paper.

Cream butter, peanut butter, sugar, and vanilla for two minutes with an electric mixer until light and fluffy.

Add egg and yolk and beat until combined.

Stir in banana.

Add flour, baking powder, baking soda, salt and mix on low until combined.

Stir in peanut butter chips and chocolate chips.

For 2.5-inch cookies, use a 1 ¾ inch diameter cookie scoop and drop about 2 inches apart on the baking sheet. For 4-inch cookies, use a ¼ cup cookie scoop.

You can add chopped peanuts and/or rainbow sprinkles to the tops of the cookies for additional flair.

Bake medium-sized cookies for about 8 minutes, or until golden brown. Bake large cookies for about 11 minutes. Allow cookies to cool on the sheets—they will be soft.

These moist, flavorful cookies are delicious warm from the oven, at room temperature, or cold straight out of the fridge or freezer. If you have extras after the first day, store them in the fridge or freeze them.

ACKNOWLEDGMENTS

This book was a lot of fun to write, and made possible by the wonderful people that help me turn a seed of an idea into an actual book. Thank you to my amazing plot group, my stalwart co-working group, my curious and energetic writing students, and to Sara Kettler for the copy edit and Tracy at Amaze Inn Proofreading for the proofread. All mistakes are my own. Thanks to Dar at Wicked Smart Designs for a beautiful autumnal cover. Special thanks to Amanda for both her enthusiasm and for the helpful beta feedback which made the book immeasurably better.

Thanks to all the readers who enjoy spending time in Rosedale.

Finally, I dedicate this book to my grandmother, who passed away shortly before publication. She was a huge reader all of her life, turning to audiobooks when her vision deteriorated due to macular degeneration. She loved to write herself, and was always supportive of my desire to write fiction. I miss her terribly, but have the comfort of many wonderful memories.

Tell those you love that you love them today.

xoxo,

Elle

ABOUT THE AUTHOR

Fueled by chocolate and canned wine, Elle Waters writes steamy small town romance with guaranteed happy endings. She lives with her family in Connecticut. Sign up for her newsletter at ellewatersauthor.com to hear about her next release!

Elle loves to hear from readers at elle@ellewatersauthor.com.

facebook.com/ElleWatersAuthor

instagram.com/ellewatersbooks

amazon.com/~/e/B091FZQ4PZ

bookbub.com/authors/elle-waters